I0693732

— **Summary** —

Jared Baylor was not the type to leave without a trace. He would never leave his job, his belongings, and his friends behind. Yet, he had been missing for three months and no one had any leads to his whereabouts. Eighteen and being the most likely to escape the small town of Lones Lake, most assumed he ran away from the fake smiles and white lies but what if he was right under their noses after all that time? What if he wasn't running away or dead like the rumors from the barflies claimed?

Husher Carden was used to living in a small town, knowing everything about everyone. Husher was trouble since he was five and accidentally threw a pie at the mayor's wife. Half-truths, rumors, and saying 'bless their heart' when someone did something stupid was a must for living in Lones Lake. As the months grew colder Husher and his friends scramble to try and find Jared before it's too late. But are they able to make it in time or is Jared Baylor going to be another missing persons case left to be forgotten?

Content Warnings

Graphic: *(Explicit, detailed description)*
Cursing, Confinement, Gaslighting, Grief, Kidnapping, Mental Illness, Panic Attacks/Disorders, Suicidal Thoughts

Moderate:
Blood, Fire/Fire injury, Injury/Injury Detail, Murder, Physical Abuse, Violence

Minor: *(Brief mention or description)*
Child Abuse (past), Death, Death of Parent (background character), Emotional Abuse (past), Fatphobia, Gun Violence

Nutrition Facts

Book Title   61,694 Words

THE MISSING VAMPIRE   24 Chapters Per Book

Amount per serving

PAGES   343

Representation	% Daily Value*
Autistic, Demisexual MC	50%
ADHD, Gay MC	50%
ADHD, Lesbian SC	25%
Autistic, Non-Binary, Aro/Ace SC	25%

Tropes

Friends to Lovers	100%
Hurt/Comfort	50%
Small Town	60%
Found Family	99%
Idiots to Lovers	100%
Angst with a Happy Ending	100%

Genre   Romance/Horror

Demographics   100%

Adult 110g

LGBTQIA+ 200g

Point of View   Duel, Third Person

* Percent daily suggested a chapter diet, your daily intake may be higher or lower depending on your reading needs

Play List

★ **BLACKOUT** by AViVA

★ **Bones** by Imagine Dragons

★ **The Dead Come Talking** by Roe Kapara

★ **Devil Town** by Cavetown

★ **Get Out Alive** by Three Days Grace

★ **Hill I Will Die On** by Alec Benjamin

★ **Hugging You** by Tom Rosenthal

★ **It's Alright** by Mother Mother

★ **Lonely Vampire** by Weathers

★ **Strawberry Mentos** by Leanna Firestone

★ **Take Me Away** by New Medicine

★ **Welcome to the Family** by Avenged Sevenfold

★ **Werewolf** by Motionless In White

★ **Who's In Control** by Set It Off

★ **Only Love Can Save Me Now** by The Pretty Reck-less

KEEP
OUT

THE MISSING VAMPIRE

DUSTIN MARS

MIDNIGHT READS
PUBLISHING

To my parents who think I hang the moon no matter how unrealistic that is.

Chapter One
Wakey Wakey

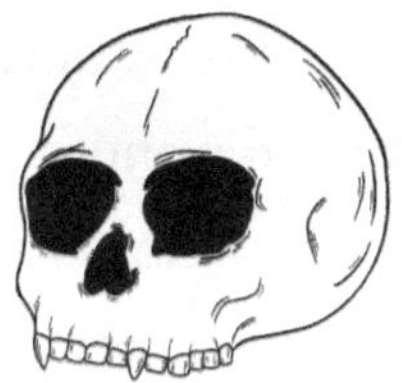

Jared Baylor – 05, September (Tuesday)

Jared knew he wasn't cut out for most of the things he did.

Like the time he convinced Husher's parents they would be fine going trick-or-treating on their own when they were twelve, and then an hour later running into Husher's house convinced the ghost from Mr. Frey's front yard was after them.

Something that was very convincing then—and when they were thirteen and thought it wouldn't happen again only to be wrapped in warm blankets and curled up on the living room couch watching comforting Halloween movies because it very much *did* happen again.

Jared also knew that him being a total clueless disaster who could barely walk and chew at the same time without seriously thinking about it, might not make for the best person to escape his current situation. He knew for sure he was *not* the person the detective would look to for answers, but rather tilt their head and wonder if he was the reason that there were instructions on the back of shampoo.

Then again, who else would it be?

Jared Baylor would be the first to say he was not made for the absolute bullshit that always seemed to find him and slap him in the face. Blatantly dead on and always managing a kick when he was down.

Just for good measure.

It didn't matter what good he did in his lifetime; the saying *no matter how good or bad things got, they would always come back to the middle,* wasn't true for Jared. It seemed like instead of the next random event being less extreme than the previous it was *more* extreme. As if the whole regression toward the mean meant nothing to him.

This, though, was the last straw. The calm before the storm, though he wasn't even all that calm—he was more high-strung than Lee was when he told them the diner was out of orange juice last summer.

He had no idea why this was happening. It was a question he didn't think he would ever get an answer to, and the longer he was there the more he wasn't all that sure he *wanted* the answer to it.

The whole thing sounded like the start of some joke. The kind of joke that no one would find funny, not even the people who doubled over at the most simplistic puns or the most basic dad jokes.

Jared was pretty sure the headline of the local paper would read something along the lines of: *"Local vampire gets lost and abducted all the while having no idea what the fuck was actually happening."*

All Jared knew was that he was cold when he woke up.

If it stopped there he would have been fine—he would have most likely chalked it up to forgetting to close his window or something equally inconsequential before he fell asleep—but no, it wasn't until he was met with the familiar and not at all comforting bitch-slap that was his luck—that he even realized that vas *not* the case.

The room he was in was dark, and despite not seeing anything around him, he knew it wasn't his room. He knew it like he knew the lines on the palm of his hand or the total number of times he declared he wouldn't bring home another plant... and failed each and every time.

Lights were strung in his room, pictures of him and his friends on the wall taken by the camera he was given last year for his birthday. There was an ivy plant that took over most of his room to the point most people thought it was fake. Plants, in general, taking over his room; the soft bedding made from dreams because it really was *that* soft, and how no matter what, his room always had a lingering scent of apple pie—from living above a diner well known for it.

Where he currently was seemed like the total opposite. As if he were kicked down a spiraling staircase that went on for all eternity.

He didn't move at first. Whether it be the paranoia of something not being quite right or his body knowing before him that it was best to fake being asleep for a moment longer, he didn't know.

At first, he heard nothing, the silence almost deafening compared to the chatter around Miss Moon's Diner, but the silence was a fleeting thing, something he wished to have back the second it was gone.

He heard whispers.

Whispers from voices he most certainly had never heard a day in his life. Maybe he was really starting to lose it. Maybe the Baylor family traits were starting to get to him after all.

The voices were getting to him much like they did his own parents.

"I'm telling you now, I am *not* covering for you again," the first voice said. It was higher pitched than the other, with no accent that Jared could detect. "If you get caught you're done, and you know it."

The other voice sent an uncomfortable chill down his spine. The chuckle felt like there was no hint of humor behind it and did nothing to help Jared's nerves at all. "We had a deal, I'm keepin' my end of it. You keep yours."

Jared opened his eyes for a moment, but it was still too dark to notice anything that could help him figure out where the actual *fuck* he was and why the hell there were two people outside his door talking about some deal.

It was like the start of one of Mason's bad horror movies she always insisted were good while Lee, Husher, and Jared all were trying *not* to look at the person on screen who had their organs on the outside of their body.

Maybe it was just a nightmare.

He had more vivid dreams before; it wasn't something he'd put past his subconscious. It would explain why the rest of the hushed whispers were just that.

He couldn't make out any of the words they were saying, the distance between whoever

was out there too much to be anything but muffled sentences at that point.

Jared tried to move around a little to wake himself up, to figure out if it was a dream or if he was awake already. He knew that in his dreams, the few times he noticed it, he never had the same amount of fingers on a hand.

All he had to do was count them. It seemed easy enough.

Feeling for his other hand in his sleep-filled haze was an easier thought than put into practice. Taking and feeling for each finger to make sure this was all just a stupid nightmare, counting five on each hand only confused him more. He felt the ring on his right hand still intact on his pointer finger. He vaguely remembered fidgeting with it the night before.

Was he wrong, was it not a dream?

If it wasn't, then what the hell was happening?!

The house creaked, making him jump a bit, the thought of having no clue where he was started to set in. All he knew was the room was dark, the couch he was laying on was smelly, and he was suddenly awfully aware that the whole thing might *not* be a nightmare?!

A door slammed shut before Jared could process anything else. He heard footsteps coming closer and closer until the door was opening and in pure panic he closed his eyes, pretending to be asleep again.

His vampire *skills* kicked in, and in typical fashion, Jared panicked and chose to play dead as if he were more possum than vampire. It was genuinely just as annoying as the freeze option of fight-or-flight.

He knew someone was walking into the room, but it was too silent to tell where they were or anything else by the sound of how they walked. He was stuck not knowing anything about them. There was a good chance that whomever it was could easily overpower him and he would be giving up his cover if he even so much as breathed a little too odd.

Jared nearly fell off the couch when he felt a hand shove his arm. His eyes snapped open in terror. He was going to die there and be stuck haunting a couch.

"You need to get up before the others find you." It was one of the voices he had heard earlier, the one *without* the slight accent.

When he didn't move he was shoved again. There was something oddly familiar about waking up in the middle of the night and being rushed out of bed. Memories of him as a kid standing in his front yard, sleepy and confused as he was ushered over to a stranger who always liked to ask too many questions. Even then Jared knew better than to answer. Watching as authorities rushed into his house, looking for things that were long hidden away from the property. His parents might have been dumb enough to start selling drugs in the first place, but they weren't stupid enough to let the authorities take any of their product.

It was a lost case then, and it felt like one now. Jared might have grown up being the laughingstock of Lones Lake, but he would not go down without a fight. It ran in his cold blood and just like his family—who felt all too much like an infectious disease, like the couch he was laying on.

Jared blinked again, getting used to the darkness around him now that the door was open and the vague outline of a person was enough for him to wish the small amount of light disappeared. He knew he wasn't quite that lucky. At least with the stream of light that was let into the room it was enough to notice the woman close to his age standing over him.

She smelled a bit like the couch, a mix of muddy water or the slush of snow on the sidewalk during winter. She had a long braid of raven hair pulled to the side, a muted brown complexion, and dark green eyes that were current-ly filled with panic...that should have gotten him up, but truthfully, what was the point?

Though by now he was far too confused to know what was best for him.

She looked worried.

Despite the baggy clothes she looked sick even as she offered out her hand to pull him up, and Jared looked at the hand as if the gesture was a trick on its own. The last he could remember he was on a walk. *What happened in the few minutes it felt like he was asleep?*

"You can't be here," she said urgently.

"Well damn, I don't exactly want to be here either," Jared couldn't help but say in a deadpanned tone.

He took her hand and let her help him up.

The ache in his joints felt stiff and all too cold for his body to regulate a normal temperature. Maybe he was out longer than he thought. His mouth was dry and it kinda felt like he was drugged when he stood up. The room spun for a moment.

The stranger was slightly taller than him, maybe by an inch or so, if he had to guess. Jared looked at the stranger this time, actively trying not to fall over onto the question-able floor. His legs felt like coffee jelly and the room kept up a dizzying spin as if he had enough caffeine to rival Lee or Mason who chugged energy drinks as if they were water.

"Where am I?" Jared asked. It seemed like a good place to start, though the urgent look she had on her face made him rethink asking anything.

She ignored his question and grabbed his wrist, her grip bruisingly tight. Jared really hated when people touched him, but it seemed pointless to point out when he could feel the terror of the stranger. He would just have to ignore the urge to peel off the skin on his arm where he could feel the person's hand on him.

"We need to get you out of here before Granny notices you," she demanded, more to herself than to Jared.

"And who the fuck is that?!"

She looked back as if he just sent dishonor on her and her cow or something. Okay, he would definitely not be getting any actual answers. One thing they could agree on, it seemed, was that Jared absolutely didn't want to meet whoever the hell *Granny* was.

"Are you stupid?" the stranger asked. "She won't let you leave if she knows you're here."

That seemed like the worst kind of hospitality, but then again, Jared only had his friends' families to compare it to. Maybe they were more of the *'we're making illegal blue stuff in the camper outback'* type and less like Husher's parents, who made sure to have oat milk stocked in the fridge at all times because Jared liked it more than whole milk.

"If I'm being honest, I kinda thought you were joking at first," Jared deadpanned.

Which only brought him back to being more confused than he was when he was forced to write in MLA formatting and failing *every* time and being gaslit by whatever not-so-mythical being was in charge of the English formatting—and who he was definitely cursed by.

Jared took note of the stranger's face and took the silent hint that she was certainly not joking about the whole thing. Which, along with the abandoned house they had going on there, it was about equally as reassuring.

"The fact I don't think you're joking is immensely not comforting," Jared informed the total stranger standing only a foot away from his face.

"I assure you I am not joking. Now let's go."

He watched as she walked over to the door and looked out into the hallway, silently listening for any movement elsewhere in the house. There must have been nothing since she was urging him to walk closer.

Jared didn't really have any other options he could think of, and the thought of staying in that room any longer was *not* what he wanted to do either. Just going with whatever was happening wouldn't be the weirdest moment of his life. At least he was *trying* to leave. That counted towards something.

He walked over to the door, but the woman put her arm out in front of him before he could walk out into the hallway. Jared stepped back from her touch; he did *not* need the extra contact from anyone until he initiated it.

"Follow where I step exactly," she whispered. "Nod if you understand."

Jared nodded.

Legitimately, he wasn't that stupid.

She looked out the door one more time before slowly stepping out, off to the left a bit rather than the center of the hallway. Jared followed, watching where she stepped. He stepped out of the dark room and slowly followed suit.

The hallway wasn't much better. The walls looked like they hadn't been dusted or painted since the house was built in the eighteen hundreds. The floor was worn, with dirt collecting near the baseboards and in the corners.

It fit the smell of the couch, and Jared did his best not to breathe through his nose too much. It was almost like the house was rotting from the inside out, or like when Husher tried to cook again even though his mom banned him from all kitchen appliances indefinitely.

Jared followed along in what felt like some of the longest few minutes of his life at the slow pace they were walking. The reality of it all had yet to set in, and all Jared could think was that they must have forgotten to pay the power bill as the hallway only grew darker and darker.

They stepped into the kitchen, a room with a few candles along the counter to light the room, and if not for the sick feeling of wanting to throw up he would have laughed at how obscure it looked. He got distracted by the mess that was on every surface, the questionable oozing-looking things on the equally revolting-looking countertop, and old newspapers draped over most of the lingering mess, but it was enough to have him misstep on his way past.

The sound of the floorboards creaking was almost enough to have him running. Instead, his body chose to freeze at his mistake.

"Shit—sorry," Jared whispered.

He knew he messed up, even without the pause the stranger gave. Her body was somehow even more tense than it was before. She looked back at him, abandoning the eerie silence to yell at him with a horror-laced voice.

"Run!"

The words took too long to process.

Jared felt himself fall to the floor before he even noticed the person behind him. The back of his head throbbed as he fought not to close his eyes. If he did, he would be done for. He knew if he didn't do something he would be deader than roadkill in July.

However, before he could help it, the world around him grew darker and darker. He couldn't help but abandon the thought as he closed his eyes.

Chapter Two
Barflies and Strawberry Waffles

When Husher tugged open the door, he was met with the comforting scent of coffee and breakfast at its best. The local diner was always busy. It didn't matter if it was seven in the morning or ten at night, the place had a charm about it no one could touch.

The door swung open behind him a few seconds later as he narrowly avoided being up close and personal with the wall and was pushed ahead by the person behind him. Then, as if that wasn't enough he was flicked in the arm for good measure.

"I told you to wait," his sister grumbled. "I had to get my other shoes since Mama forgot to tell me she washed my other ones."

The Carden siblings each took after a different parent both in looks and personality. While Husher was four years older, he was known for all the pranks he pulled while in middle school. However, his sister, Ava, was best known for her accomplishments much like their mom. Ava had brown eyes that reminded Husher of oak rather than the hazel green eyes he had. Her skin was a warm umber brown and her hair so dark it might as well have been the midnight sky. While Husher was tanner than most in town, his dirty blond hair was a dead giveaway as to which parent he took his looks from.

Ava shoved past him as she walked over to one of the few open tables. The diner itself was on the smaller side, tables pushed together leaving just enough room for people to walk past and not much more space than that. The diner's layout changed daily with the amount of groups that pushed tables together as needed or a few who just wanted their usual table but in a different spot.

Husher looked around the diner for a moment, gazing at all the artwork hung on the walls from the owner's years traveling before she moved back home to take over the business when her parents died. The place was cozy, and other than the placement of the tables and chairs, nothing really ever changed about it. No matter how much the mayor and her wife tried to push near the holidays for some decorations, Miss Moon was a stubborn woman when she wanted to be and won that argument every time.

"I really need everyone to stop referring to each *Heather* as their aesthetic color," Ava muttered. She set her phone on the table, apparently frustrated with her group chat again.

"Why? The red one's my favorite," Husher teased.

Ava flipped him off.

"We aren't even casting them until next week and no one can even learn their *actual* names," Ava muttered.

Husher had never been overly into musicals even in school, having more interest in finding a stick while on a walk and poking something with it. His sister, on the other hand, had signed up for the school musical yet again. Another year Husher would end up learning every song—much to his own protest, and being dragged to every show would be the death of him and his *Spotify-wrapped* list.

The waitress, Eve, didn't bother asking what they wanted but rather set their usual drinks in front of them. "The usual or the sugar rush usual?"

"Sugar rush usual," Husher answered without hesitation, because he seriously needed his comfort food.

"Why am I not surprised," Eve sighed. "Alrighty, strawberry waffles." She then looked over to Ava. "And an egg sandwich?"

Ava nodded. "Yep, that works for me."

"Thank you," Husher smiled.

"Yeah, yeah," Eve waved him off.

Husher turned back to his sister, who was taking a break from managing the school play and instead took a sip of her lemonade. Husher cringed at the drink. Lemonade was never sweet enough even with the pound of sugar they added to it.

"You're still working on the set?" Husher asked. He picked up the straw he was given before throwing the wrapper to his sister, only for her to throw it right back at him, nearly hitting him in the eye.

"Yeah, we have the designs drawn, but we're waiting to build everything," Ava informed him. "Oh, and Mom signed you up to help her with building some of the stage."

"The highlight of my week."

She nodded. Whether she got the note of sarcasm laced into his words, Husher didn't know.

He watched out of the window. People he had known his whole life, people who were visiting to see the colorful November trees and/or visiting the local shops known for their autumn aesthetics, cozy drinks, and the perfect small town shopping center this time of year.

Everything was so normal, it was off-putting.

The way the town rushed so quickly to get back to their routines, their own lives, as if there wasn't anything wrong. As if someone hadn't gone missing for *sixty-two days* and counting. He knew just because he was sinking, that it didn't mean everyone else had to be as well. He knew that they weren't plagued with the fact their best friend had suddenly vanished, leaving behind everything and everyone.

No note, no plan, no proof that it was a runaway, yet, most believed it to be just that.

Husher knew better.

He knew better than to think the rumors were anything but that. Lies spread like wildfire in small towns.

Ava was on her phone again messaging the rest of the drama club before Miss Moon could catch her. The '*No Phones*' sign was posted behind the main counter and again near the counter with all the baked goods, but Miss

Moon usually didn't mind as long as you made it quick or took the call outside.

Husher was lost in thought until the whispers around him started again.

Growing up in Lones Lake, it was nothing new to him. He had caused trouble as a kid, too much not to have a few whispers about him. High school might have been over a year ago for him, but he felt like he was still there with the way people around him gossiped.

He was pretty sure high schoolers cared less about gossip than the people currently talking in a loud whisper not even two tables away from him.

Though, this time, the gossip wasn't about who he kissed when he was fifteen and playing spin the bottle just before the party got shut down. This time it felt much more personal than any peck on the lips with his science partner ever could.

He tried not to listen to the barflies and regulars who were getting their breakfast; the people known for always having the worst things to say. They were worse than walking past a group of middle schoolers who no matter what always knew his deepest insecurities as if he wore them on his sleeve.

"They still didn't find that kid," the one guy muttered.

The man beside him chuckled. "Probably dead at this point. There ain't no way anyone is surviving out there now, bloodsucker or not."

"Yeah, you're probably right." The first guy shook his head. "Shame, though."

Husher glared back at them, but what was the point? They didn't look up from their conversation to see the glare sent their way from the town's resident sunshine dude. It took something personal for Husher who must have been blessed by someone's southern grandma at some point in his life to actively wish someone their bad karma early.

"You can't listen to those assholes," Eve muttered.

She set down their food, and the extra whipped cream and strawberries on Husher's dish didn't go unnoticed. He thought most of the regulars at the diner felt the same as he did. The crushing feeling that something was horribly wrong. Glaring daggers to the barflies who had nothing better than to add their worthless two cents about the situation.

Jared was not just someone who was there one day and gone like the people visiting their town on vacation. He was one of them, a friend to most, or family to some.

"They gossip worse than anyone I've ever heard, and most of it comes out of their ass," Ava chimed in.

"Wow, super helpful," Husher muttered.

"No cursing in the *damn* diner," Eve muttered, ignoring her own statement. "Now eat before it gets cold." And with that, she walked away to deal with a group of vacationers Husher didn't recognize.

Husher sighed and ate the waffles, the strawberry glaze and whipped cream doing nothing to help settle his stomach like it usually did.

"You know Samuel will get a lead, he won't stop looking," Ava muttered.

Husher logically knew she was right, but it just didn't seem to make a difference when he tried to think about it. Sure, he understood Samuel would keep looking. He knew just like anyone who had ever met the sheriff that he would try his best. However, the fact it had been well over a month alone was enough to feel a bit hopeless about the whole thing. The constant weight on his shoulders, pushing him farther down into a pit of depression.

Instead, he took another bite and nodded.

They would get somewhere with it all, he just didn't know if it would be too late.

He cleared the table the best he could once they were done, paid, and he was back to his crushing thoughts as he walked out of the diner.

"I have a half-day so I'm stopping at the store on my way home. Do you want those strawberry candies?"

Husher simply nodded.

"Okay, see ya then," Ava flicked his arm before they went their separate ways. Ava headed to school and Husher to work.

The blond walked back home to get his work supplies only to drive down the road. He could have walked, but lugging all the supplies was not something he liked doing if he could help it. There was too much for one person anyway. Usually, he worked with his mom. However, she was dealing with a migraine that morning, so he told her he would just do their usual clients since it was an easy day on their schedule and she could take her migraine medication and rest.

He arrived at the first house, using the spare key the owner had recently given him. He got to work cleaning the ranch-style house from top to bottom, dusting, sweeping, and mopping everything he usually did.

The first house was fine. Doing all the work himself took a little longer, but he made good time getting to his next client just a few blocks away. In the second house, he wasn't as lucky. Mrs. Bell was an older lady who followed him from room to room telling him all about whatever it was she felt the need to talk about that day, one of the few old white ladies who didn't give him the creeps and who always made the best sugar cookies in December. Though this particular day she must have been reading the local paper, something he didn't think people used for more than shredding up for their animal's litter boxes or for a makeshift drop cloth when painting theater props.

"It would be awful out there," she started. "Last night it was nearly freezing out. I think it was thirty-four degrees Fahrenheit out or about one degree Celsius when I last looked."

"I didn't notice," Husher muttered, like the polite liar he seemed to be becoming.

He knew the temperature would only get worse. Winter in Pennsylvania was just like any other season. One day it would be raining and reaching nearly freezing temperatures, the next it was the end of December and he was wearing shorts and a t-shirt.

"Well, I think they just need to look harder. I mean what the hell are they doing all day anyway," Mrs. Bell grumbled.

"I'm sure most of them are working on important things," Husher lied again.

He did *not* want to talk her down from going into the police station *again* with a box of pig-themed donuts. Husher could only hope to be like that when he got older. Old enough he could get away with that kind of thing.

Then again, he knew people like him usually didn't get brushed off as easily as people like Mrs. Bell. It was never an issue for an innocent old white lady to say or do whatever she wanted. Mrs. Bell took pride in making others uncomfortable when they annoyed her.

"Bullshit," the old woman chuckled. "We're taking care of things ourselves anyway."

Husher simply nodded and continued cleaning, making it easier to just go through his routine with each room at a time. Listening to her ramblings and wanting to be left alone the entire time.

"So Marly decided she didn't want the dog any more so she was asking around for someone to take the poor little thing," Mrs. Bell sighed. "I told her to call over to the Nelson's and their youngest happily took it."

Husher was rushing to clean the last room, dusting around the window before grabbing the vacuum. "Well that's good they know you then," Husher agreed with her.

"Everyone is," she shrugged. "I'd love to have me as a friend."

He finished up there and moved on to the next house that was just out of town a few miles. He ate a quick lunch before he got there, and much like the last house, the owner was home and the rumors were just as bad. Husher just wanted to crawl into bed and rot for a few hours, days maybe; if it meant he could have a moment of peace. The rumors only spiraled to half-truths and absurd accusations. He wanted to scream, to cry, to maybe even ask a witch about cursing a few of them. There was nothing good from gossip, especially when someone's life was tied to the end of the rumor someone was trying to pass as the truth.

"I'm just saying you'd tell them if you heard anything, right?"

Husher was pretty sure he was the calmest of his friend group, the one who picked a peaceful ending over a tragic one in the few video games he played. However, comments like this made him want to scream in rushed phrases his mama reserved for when her family visited for the holidays.

"Yes, I've already done that," Husher managed.

He was at work. He did not need to go off on someone, and he wasn't Mason—he didn't throw wrenches at people first and deny questions later. He needed to finish cleaning the bathroom and then he could sweep, mop, and leave.

Husher did just that, nodding along to what the old dude was saying and never being so happy to hear the loud sound of a vacuum cleaner in his life.

He finished up the house and took his check before driving back home.

He didn't know what was worse: when the clients told him rumors as if they witnessed the events or when they gave him pitying looks—looks of sadness as if they knew something he didn't, something that he thought might be true but didn't want to believe.

He pulled into the driveway, fumbling with the garage door remote for a few seconds knowing full well he needed to get new batteries for it before it stopped working altogether. He parked the car in the garage and sat there for a moment, the car off as he pressed the button for the garage door to go down. He didn't bother getting the dirty rags out of the car, he didn't bother cleaning any of the cleaning supplies out yet. It was a task that could wait for later. He stepped inside with a sigh that would have landed him the lead to any play the drama club was performing.

His mama greeted him first. "Rough day, mijo?"

He walked over to the couch and lay face down. It wasn't the worst day he had in a while, but nowhere near to being good.

"It's worse than the day I hit the mayor's wife with a damn pie," he said into the cushion.

"Well, you did manage to do it *twice* in the same day," Ava added helpfully.

His mom looked up from what she was cooking, the smell of garlic and herbs filling the house pleasantly. Ava was helping her since she was the only one allowed to. His mom tried to teach him, but apparently starting one—or ten—too many small fires was enough to ban him.

His mama sighed and patted him on the back. He swore it was genetic, because he fully took after her when it came to their cooking skills, leaving them both banned from doing anything other than the cleanup in the kitchen.

"You know how they are," his mama tried. "Once something takes their interest, they will be talking about it as if it directly affected them."

Husher remained flopped on the couch. "I had to listen to Mrs. Bell tell me about the weather for an hour."

"And you'll let her, we are not missing her sugar cookies," his mama informed him.

"Dawn, sweetheart, love of my life," his mom started. "Get over what happened last year, I said I was sorry!"

Last year just before the gift-wrapped boxes of cookies were sent out, Husher's mom *might* have made a comment to Mrs. Bell about the choice of wrapping paper laying on the kitchen counter not being appropriate. Husher kinda thought it was funny, a pattern of little middle fingers with holly all over the wrapping paper was iconic in a way, however, his mama had still not gotten over it even if Ava and their mom made sugar cookies the night they knew they would *not* be getting Mrs. Bell's. It just wasn't the same.

"Sure, sure, but if I have another year and no cookies, it is not going to be a good one for anyone," his mama assured them.

Which Husher had to agree with. He wanted those cookies just as much as she did, and he would never mess that up. There was just no one who could recreate them. Miss Moon would be close, but even then Husher didn't know if it was possible.

Husher lay there for a while longer before finally getting up and cleaning out the car for the next day, replacing rags and putting the dirty ones in the washer in the garage specifically for their cleaning supplies.

By the time he was done, he went in and ate dinner, zoning out for most of it. His family seemed to get the hint to not push him this time. He cleared his plate and helped his mama clean the kitchen before he headed over to his room.

He felt drained, and while being around people usually helped him, today seemed to feel like the opposite.

He couldn't help the rushing thoughts that Jared had to have left something behind. Some kind of clue to tell him where he went. There had to be something he wasn't seeing.

Just what the hell was it?

WOULDN'T YOU LIKE TO KNOW *middle finger emoji*
MaSoN – 19:48

WHY DO PEOPLE SUCK SO MUCH??

PUTAS :/

WE SHOULD JUST GO

Husher was used to his friend's messages by now. Mason never talked in anything but capital letters—something she managed to do in face-to-face conversations as well. He didn't need to be told what the message meant either.

They had been going back and forth with whether they should visit Jared's bio parents to see if they somehow had something to do with his disappearance. Husher doubted it would be of any help; they all knew Jared's bio parents were a waste of space.

Why would they be helpful for this?

His phone chimed as soon as he sat it down. He picked it back up again, unlocked it, and read the latest message from the group chat.

Husher at least had Lee on his side for thinking it was a terrible idea. It wasn't like the thought wasn't there. Anything would be more helpful than nothing.

Husher flopped back on his bed, the familiar helpless feeling sinking into his body with each second that passed by. He had no idea what to do and felt like he had tried everything already.

It was like Jared Baylor never existed at all.

Chapter Three
Welcome to the Family...

Jared Baylor – 09, November (Thursday)

J ared was used to the routine by now. Weeks of trying to get through the day without running into any of the family members who always seemed to know where he was, deemed challenging at first.

Staying awake until he passed out just so he could do it, again and again, day after day was equally as challenging.

He would sleep for only a few hours, get up, and walk around in the sunlight to get his body temperature up—the house was colder inside than the few times he managed to get a window open. Being able to breathe in air that didn't smell like a shit filled dump, helped clear his head ever so slightly.

Jared waited a moment, listening for any sounds downstairs. He knew the Graham family had no set routine, other than when they would cook. Brandy was in the attic, where she stayed most of the time. Jared didn't see her all that much, but when he did, it only made the hope of getting out of there dwindle away. Terry was normally outside by this time. Jordan was unpredictable and more like a ticking time bomb when he was in the house. Granny should have been asleep or outside; the lack of noise confirmed that. Though one wrong move or misjudged decision and he would pay for it.

Slowly, he made his way downstairs. Old creaky steps that looked way too much like something out of a horror movie for Jared's liking. Much like the rest of the farm-style house, it looked old, and Jared felt as if one wrong step would either give his hiding spot away or he would fall into the pits of Tartarus—the basement. The kitchen was covered in thick layers of dust so impressive Jared had to question how it was real. The countertops and the kitchen table were covered in dirty dishes. Food scattered about, some rotting, some with bugs crawling out of it, home to countless bacteria and undiscovered diseases.

Mornings—late mornings were the best time to try to find something edible. By then the breakfast was over, and Granny was off in the garden—though Jared didn't know what she could be doing to a garden in November, but he left it alone.

She was out of the house and that was enough.

"Is she ever going to realize there isn't anything growing out there?" Jared asked as Cheryl crept into the room.

The view from the window above the sink was limited at best, the screen ripping away. In the kitchen, there were a few things that weren't rotting away or turning into the questionable mess on the floor or counters. Cans of fruit were left hidden in cabinets, cans that looked old enough to most likely not have touched the state of the rest of the kitchen. Besides being covered in layers of dust, the cans were in decent condition given the broken and greasy cabinets.

"No," Cheryl answered. "She never does. It snows and she goes out there just like any other day."

"Great, so the chances of her freezing to death out there is low?" Jared questioned before he grabbed a glass jar of what looked like peaches and made sure the seal was intact before quietly opening it.

Cheryl nodded. "Low. I've locked her out, but she finds a way in. She is used to the cold by now."

"Fucking peachy." Jared left it at that and headed back upstairs.

In the beginning, it had taken some getting used to. Cheryl, the woman that had tried to get him out of the house before Granny found him, was the only one who tried to help him. She had informed him about staying out of Granny's way, and how the old hag's temper was worse and worse each time. Jared stayed out of *everyone's* way. He didn't have to be told twice to do it either. He was good at hiding, good at being forgettable, but he was not good at figuring out how the fuck to get out of the shithole without being caught or killed.

Starving in a house of humans was not a highlight, having to breathe unknown herbs that made it revolting to even think about feeding on them was another thing to the highlights. It wasn't like he fed from the vein anyway. Vampires always got a bad rep for it, plus the synthetic blood was more nutritious.

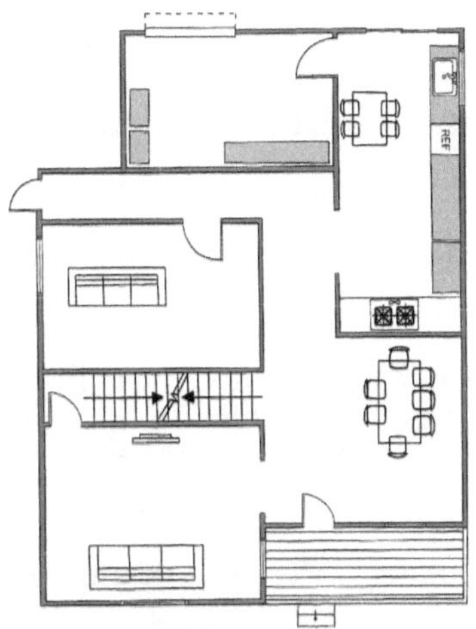

*Main Floor of the Graham
Family House*

Looking around the house, he knew there was most likely some generational curse or maybe just an awfully unlucky family bloodline. The main floor of the house had a small living room near the kitchen. Painted in soft blue, he thought, before the years of dust and death coated them. The dining room and kitchen were somehow worse. Grease covered most of the kitchen, and slimy sludge sat in what Jared assumed was the sink. Looking back to just about any horror movie that involved an old farmhouse seemed fitting. The layout was simple, and at one point the furniture might have passed for good. Though now,

Jared wasn't sure it passed for anything other than a disease test. Surprisingly, there was an old TV sitting on a nearly collapsing table; a TV that someone most likely sat in front of and could feel the static from the screen. Of course, it didn't work anymore, but at this point, he wasn't sure they even noticed.

There was a small office down the hall from the kitchen, it was the room he woke up in and also the room Sabrina used as a playroom and would scream if anyone wandered in without knocking. Effective but annoying when Jared was sleeping.

Up the stairs, there were four bedrooms and a bathroom, though they were not much of an improvement from downstairs. Jared didn't know where Granny actually slept or if she even slept at all. She kinda just disappeared for a while and Jared didn't need to know the reason why or even where she went as long as it was away from him.

The master bedroom was always locked and was the only room that led to the attic. Jared picked the lock one time, but seeing Brandy rocking herself in the middle of the room was enough not to be looking around again.

Cheryl gave him the rundown of the family, but Jared was too sick to care. The first room up the steps was Jordan's. The oldest son and the kind of person that Jared was pretty sure that if searched online Jordan would be the first to show up on some kind of list for reasons not to have children. Jordan Graham was twenty-seven, though given the living conditions, he looked much older than that. The lingering smell of moldy socks wafted out of the room much like it did when Jared was in the same room as the dude. The brunet was around Mason's height, Jared guessed he was around five-foot-nine, and was one of the few people that made Jared look tan in comparison. Jordan was too much like a middle school bully who constantly took things too far, from the ugly-ass baseball hats to the even shittier personality. Jared was surprised the dickhead wasn't dead yet, though he had the time to hope.

The next room was Sabrina's, the youngest of the Graham family and the only one who might have a chance at living a decent life if she got out of the house from Hell. Sabrina was four-foot-nine. Jared had noticed the height markers outside her door one day. It was something he knew most parents did with their kids but it seemed strange for the Graham family to care for such things so he assumed Cheryl kept up with it. While Jared tended to avoid children like the summer sun, Sabrina seemed to act a lot younger than any eleven-year-old Jared had the misfortune of meeting. She, much like the rest of the Graham family, had brown hair, eyes to match, and paler-than-the-moon level pigment. Her long hair was matted in the back—despite Cheryl's best attempts to fix it but without any kind of conditioner or brushes there wasn't much she could do other than cut it—which apparently was *not* happening.

The last room in the hallway was empty—well, it was left for storage, filled with what looked like trash and smelled a lot like it too. Though, once Jared got used to the smell he was able to work around it. Finding a few good hiding spots from the family when he needed them. It was best for him to just stay hidden and out of sight most days.

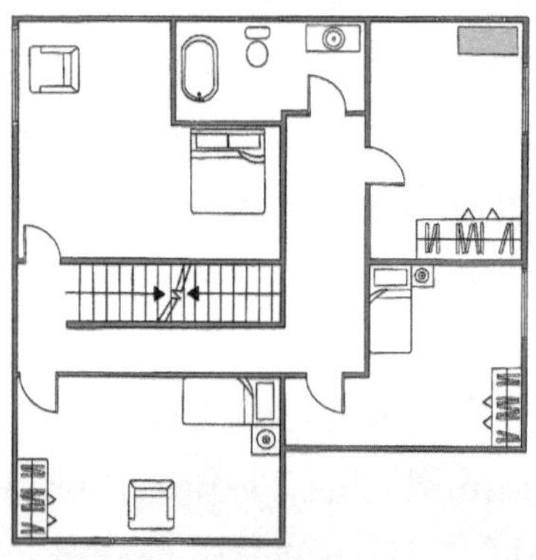

Upstairs of the Graham Family House

The house could have been nice. Maybe it once was, back when it was built and the people who lived there had empathy and their full state of mind intact. However, now it looked like total shit.

Out of the whole thing, the basement was the worst. Jared tried to never go down there again. The damp earthy smell mixed with rotting meats was enough for him to vomit on the steps leading down there. Boredom and the curious thought of it leading to a way out he tried again. The basement was always dark, built of mainly concrete from what Jared explored, it was like a never-ending maze of confusing hallways and rooms that led him into other rooms, all filled with useless shit. It all looked like a place where the main victim was dragged down there never to escape. Jared always was on edge down there, the hair on his arms would stand up, shivers were sent down his spine, and each time he went down there it felt like he wouldn't come back. The basement was never going to be a place he would want to go. The whole thing made him feel like he was living out his life as the first victim in one of the True Crime podcasts he tended to listen to. The dumbass who thought the sound was something to be walked toward and not away from. Jared might have been white, but he was *not* that fucking white.

In the living room, there was a door leading down to the basement. Cheryl had learned where to go and how to hide in her own way. Down the steps, there was a cement room, with no windows, the only light coming in was from a hole in the floor above and various candles.

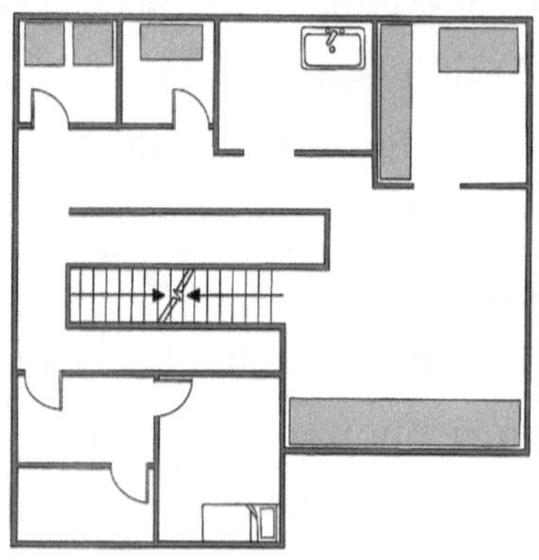

Basement of the Graham Family
House

The first room was filled with meats, improperly stored, and rotting flesh of what looked to once be a form of cattle. Jared tried *not* to look. Then there was a smaller room that definitely looked like something out of a horror movie involving a house and way too much fucking wax. Down the hallway, there were a few smaller rooms. Jared peeked into each room carefully, mountains of trash was piling up from what he assumed were decades of throwing things to the ground, in storage boxes, any place they could get it shoved out of the way.

Spiders covered everything, and while Jared never overly minded bugs—growing up with Husher, who was absolutely terrified of them, Jared was used to trapping and releasing them, especially in the spring and autumn seasons—but this was a bit more than he was comfortable with.

The family dinners were what got Jared to his breaking point and with each dinner he never quite knew how he was going to recover. He did his best to avoid the family but it wasn't always a foolproof thing. Hiding where he could as he wandered the house. Though from time to time Jared messed up. This time he knew the second he stepped out of his hiding spot, he knew he had misjudged it. He fucked up and there was no way out of it. His arm was yanked forward, and soon enough he found himself being pulled away from the area he was hiding in, the place he thought was safe enough, hidden behind a sizable pile of boxes.

It had been hours and he needed to get out of the room. He needed to walk around before his feet froze to his shoes.

Being a vampire in the colder seasons was just as shitty as the warmer ones. It was a constant game of making sure he was getting enough sunlight to move but not so much where he would be poisoned.

However, this time when he went to move from his hiding spot he failed to listen to the house around him, failing to hear the thud of footsteps approaching him. Terry was waiting for him out in the hall and it was too late to hide again.

He was shoved into a chair. Around the table, the whole family sat. All eyes were on him for a moment watching as he panicked. They made him feel even smaller than he was.

"You best eat your food," Terry warned him.

Jared was nearly thrown a brown-looking plate with some kind of cold stew over the top, slimy and with a smell to rival the Graham family body odor. Cheryl looked over for a moment, and while it was reassuring that he wasn't totally alone, the feeling didn't last.

What made the dinners so disquieting were the lines of reality that seemed to blur. The uncooked or overcooked roadkill they managed to find was forced into his face much like the smells that were so embedded in the house, Jared didn't think that burning the place down could even help with it. All plans of poisoning the Graham family died out when Jared looked down at his plate and then around the table. Watching in disgust as everyone else shoveled the repugnant meal into their mouths. If they were happy to eat even half the shit on the plate in front of them, what good would poison do?

Jared knew he didn't want to be one of them. He knew he had to keep his mind guarded. He was not going to be another brainwashed idiot of Granny's making. The whole family seemed to follow her and what she said, like some weird cult leader Jared heard about in a podcast. The sick glint in her eyes made Jared sink into his chair. Even Jordan was eerily compliant at dinner. Cheryl had informed him the third night there that when Jordan first moved in with Granny he was worse—something that Granny would not tolerate. Cheryl had explained that if Jordan wouldn't listen to Granny, then a finger or toe was cut off by her dull butcher knife. His pinky finger and two toes were the cost of his ignorance and the price of Granny's love. Jared didn't want to know the price for non-family members.

Jared had wanted to ask why Brandy and/or Terry would let Granny take control, but he nearly laughed at that thought. They weren't much better.

He didn't know the half of it.

Jared knew all eyes were on him, engulfing him in panic. Making him feel even smaller than he was.

Cheryl had been there for years. She wasn't like Brandy; she would leave if she could. The thing about it was that every chance she had to escape, she was found every time she tried. Teaming up with her hadn't done anything so far either.

He *couldn't* end up like her.

He wouldn't.

Part of him hoped to die. The other part of him urged him to get out of there. This wouldn't be his ending. He didn't work his ass off to get through high school just for this to be how it fucking ended. He had his own family to see. A life, an actual future for once, and a promise of something good finally fucking happening.

It was just another rug pulled out from under him. Another lie he told himself to get through what was another shitty day, a shitty week, a shitty month, a year, his life. He was tired of always having to fight for himself. Having to find a small positive only to be met with a colossal negative.

While Jared knew his family would look for him, part of him was scared of what they would find.

Husher wouldn't stop until he was found—but what if there wasn't anything left to find? What if when he did find him, it was only a body?

Jared *needed* to get out before that could happen.

Chapter Four
Gone

Husher Garden – 06, September
(Wednesday)

T he day felt wrong.

Husher had no idea why, but the moment he woke up he knew something wasn't right. He went about his day as he normally would and called Jared as he got ready. Something they always did, talking before they had to get ready for work. Mostly about nothing, dreams of being taken by *The Lizard King*, or the one time Husher had informed his best friend about the time they were dragons and flying around town as one did.

Jared not picking up the phone was another thing to add to the list of things that didn't seem right. For a moment Husher thought Mason had moved everything in his room a little to the left—over the span of two months before he even noticed—*again,* but his room was untouched, and since starting to work full-time at the garage, she hadn't had time to do much else.

"Husher, take the dogs out before you leave!" his mama yelled.

He nodded then remembered she couldn't see him, but she was already heading out the door by the time he was walking out to the living room. He shrugged it off and headed back to his room and got ready for the day before he did as he was told, letting his two dogs out. Rooty, a three-year-old golden retriever, and Marco, a six-year-old blond chihuahua.

The dogs happily followed him around the house so it always made the task of letting them out much easier.

"Come on, Rooty. Marco, let's go, buddy." Husher moved out of their way to let them out the door that led out to the backyard.

Husher waited for them to come back in before locking up the house and making sure everything was secure before heading out to the garage to meet his mom. He called a few more times, but Jared didn't pick up his phone.

He walked out of the garage ignoring the fact he had to be at work in fifteen minutes.

"Where are you going?" Husher's mom asked.

"Jared's, I'll be back before we have to leave."

Husher jogged into town, knowing he was being ridiculous but it was something his stupid wolf brain wouldn't let go. Something he learned not to ignore, like a gut instinct or overwhelming uneasiness—so Husher stopped by the diner to make sure he wasn't mad at him for skipping out on a walk last night. He needed to be up early, and while it was the perfect September weather for a walk around town, he had been tired. Husher didn't think he was mad, but Jared usually had his phone charged, so it wasn't likely that it was dead.

Husher knocked on the diner door ten minutes before opening hour, but he knew Miss Moon would be in the kitchen getting everything ready for the morning rush. A few moments later a chubby woman who was only slightly taller than Jared walked out, her gray hair had streaks of lavender peaking out even as she kept it pulled back into a bun. The seventy-year-old was quite possibly the only person—besides his family—that Husher knew to be unapologetically herself. She always managed to look like a witch all year around, and growing up there were many rumors about her magic.

Going into the diner alone at night would only end with a kid being turned into a stew.

Though by now people knew her instead as the owner of the diner that nearly everyone went to on the daily. Her stormy gray eyes looked out the glass door confused to see Husher there, though she unlocked the door anyway. Her sleeves were rolled up, the tattoos of moon phases on her left arm peeking out, and flour marked the front of her black shirt and apron already.

"Husher, you know I won't open the diner any sooner," Miss Moon said in lieu of a greeting.

"I was just coming to see why Jared was ignoring my calls," Husher muttered.

He felt ridiculous. *Just because his best friend wasn't answering him, he had to show up at his house?* Even though he knew Jared would have to physically lose his phone or be dead not to answer it, Husher still felt like he was being a bit ridiculous.

"If this is like the time you pranked me when you were ten, I'm not playing along. I'm still finding blue glitter," Miss Moon answered.

Referring to the time Jared and he thought it would be fun to prank each other by wrapping their birthday gifts with glitter, confetti, and anything that once opened would explode everywhere.

"What?" Husher shook his head. "No, he isn't picking up his phone and I wanted to make sure he was okay before I went to work."

Miss Moon only looked more confused. She frowned for a moment before speaking, the feeling of something not being quite right about the situation came back full force.

"I thought he was with you," she muttered.

"No, he went for a walk to clear his head and I told him I had to get up early, so I didn't go with him," Husher told her. He left out how he woke up worried and how odd Jared had been acting last night. "It's silly," Husher scratched the back of his neck. "I just wanted to make sure he wasn't mad at me or anything for not going with him. I think he might have wanted someone to talk to, but I was too tired to really notice it at the time."

"So he didn't tell you yet," Miss Moon muttered, low enough Husher almost didn't catch it. "I just thought he stayed at your house and forgot to call me. He never came back last night."

It was Husher's turn to look confused.

First of all, he had no idea what Jared had to tell him. They had been friends long enough to know when one of them wanted to talk. Both were a bit stubborn—Jared especially—so Husher always made sure to make it easy for him and start the conversation.

And second—when Husher was able to move on to the rest of what Miss Moon had said he had a difficult time processing it. She thought he stayed over and forgot to call...

He never came back home.

"He said he was just walking around the block," Husher muttered more to himself than to Miss Moon. When he looked up at her, he saw the same worried confusion on her face that he had felt all morning.

She opened the door, letting him in, and they both rushed to the apartment above the diner, going to the back and up the stairs. Miss Moon usually kept it unlocked since no one ever bothered to explore the off limit parts of the diner, a simple *employees only* sign did the trick.

When they both made their way into the apartment and over to Jared's room it looked untouched.

Empty.

Husher looked around, but the man was nowhere in sight. Everything was still in place, his bed was unmade as it usually was. There wasn't anywhere to hide in his room. Under the bed was storage, the closet was filled with clothes, and the many windows on the front wall let in enough light to see that he wasn't there.

"And you're not fucking pranking me?" Miss Moon asked. And yep, that was very much the person who raised Jared, or at the very least where he got his colorful language from.

Husher shook his head.

Part of him wanted to ask if *she* was pranking him because none of this made any sense. Jared had just gone for a walk in a town he grew up in, then disappeared somewhere in the middle of that?

Just gone.

Husher tried to think if Jared had said anything else last night before he walked off, but his mind was blank. They walked around a lot at night. It was usually when he and Husher had free time, and walking Rooty and Marco was something Husher often got tasked with, so Jared took one of the dogs—Rooty always ran over to him, his tail hitting Husher in the leg and Marco in the face.

However, now that he thought about it, Jared had seemed a bit off last night. It seemed like he was jittery about something Husher normally would have noticed sooner. This time he hadn't picked up on the odd behavior until he thought about it along with all the little tells Jared had.

He knew Jared was used to keeping things to himself, and trying to get him to reach out when something was bothering him was nearly impossible. Husher had gotten used to it and learned how to read his best friend so he could help him without it seeming like a burden, which Jared often thought he was. He didn't give away much, his body language often giving no signs that anything was wrong. However, his clothes always did. The placement of his rings, the red one especially. If the ring was on his thumb or middle finger, he was fine. If it was on his ring finger he was annoyed, and if it was on his pointer finger he was anxious about something. Husher didn't think Jared even knew he did this, but the man unknowingly did the same thing with his hoodies. Jared seemed to group his hoodies together. Knowing him since elementary school, Husher knew Jared only wore dark clothes. Jared might have had more black hoodies than space in his closet, but they all meant something different. The logos or the memories behind them were the key to knowing what kind of mood he was in. And last night, Jared was wearing one Husher had put in the '*comfort*' hoodie category.

"He was wearing a flannel hoodie."

The hoodie Jared stole from him in high school when Husher outgrew it and then had sewn a flannel onto it because it was '*a shitty boring mess,*' so he obviously needed to alter it.

Miss Moon frowned before trying to call Jared herself. When he didn't answer she took a breath and Husher was about one minor inconvenience away from freaking out.

"Go to work," she told him. "I will keep calling him and I will let you know about any updates."

"You know just as well as I do, he would answer his phone," Husher stated. He had no idea what else to say. All his brain could do was supply him with what were the worst explanations.

"If it doesn't work I'll try a locating spell," she sighed.

As much as he didn't want to leave, she left no room for argument. He nodded and walked back down to the diner.

Jared would be fine. There are a lot of reasons why someone couldn't pick up their phone. He might have just gone to get something early and his phone died. Husher knew it made no sense, but he needed something to latch on to. The little hope that he was sorely lacking, dwindling away at an alarming rate. He just didn't know what could have happened and it was beyond bothersome.

Jared wouldn't have just up and left, and he surely wouldn't have left all his things behind.

The next day wasn't any better.

Things were only made worse when he got a message from Miss Moon to accompany her to the police station to file a missing person report.

The authorities were from the small town and knew Jared just as well as most town folks did. He worked at the diner everyone went to. They watched him grow up, they knew his biological parents, they knew he *wasn't* like them, and they knew he would *never* run away, not now at least.

Yet, Husher found himself sitting in front of one of the deputy's desks where he was fighting the urge to hit the man with the pen he had been clicking for the last four minutes.

"He's eighteen," Joel, the deputy, muttered. "He probably left. Probably knew it was about time."

Joel Smith had relocated to Lones Lake a few years ago when he moved in with his girlfriend Stephanie Fisher, who worked in the hair salon as long as Husher could remember. He was just as annoying then as he was now.

"I am telling you he is missing," Husher said again.

It had been over an hour and Husher didn't understand why they were still at square one. Joel might not have been the best to work with, but he wasn't *that* bad at his job.

"The first forty-eight to seventy-two hours are the most important. Kindly stop wasting it," Miss Moon said sternly.

That got through to him. He picked up his phone and dialed a number before leaning back in his chair.

"I'm going to need you to get back from lunch sooner than later. I have two residents insisting the Baylor kid is missing," Joel told whoever he was on the phone with.

Without another word, he hung up.

Husher watched as the man looked just as unimpressed as before. "Sheriff will be back soon, you can talk with him. Now if you don't mind, I have work to actually do."

Husher wanted to ask if it was cleaning off the sprinkles from the donut he still had stuck to the front of his uniform, but he bit back his comment. It likely wouldn't end well for him.

Miss Moon, on the other hand, noticed too.

"Thank you for your help, Joel. Feel free to stop by the diner sometime, I know how much you like those sprinkled donuts." She looked down at his shirt and back to his reddening face before giving him a smile neither of them believed.

They waited for the sheriff only a few minutes before telling him everything they told deputy Smith. Sheriff Samuel Fox led them to his office before taking notes on the information given.

"Since he's eighteen and not a minor I'm assuming the risk level we're dealing with is low?" Samuel questioned.

While Husher wanted to argue it was still just as important, he knew Samuel didn't mean anything behind his words. He was there to help them not start an argument. Husher just needed to help add to what Miss Moon was telling him and keep any rude comment to himself.

"When and where was Jared last seen?"

"Last night, about nine at the town square. We were just walking around before I went home, but he said he'd probably walk a little longer. I assumed he just meant walking around the block again," Husher told him.

"And it was just you two, no Lee or Mason?" Samuel asked.

Husher shook his head. "No, Mason was working still, and Lee was watching their cousins."

The sheriff nodded.

"Do you know if Jared had his phone, keys, money, or medications with him?" Samuel continued. Reading off the questions that only made it sink in more that Husher was having to file an actual missing persons case for his best friend.

Jared would never do this on purpose. While the crime in small towns was far from anything major, crime, in general, wasn't totally absent. Husher just didn't understand what was even happening.

"He should have had his phone. He never remembers his keys, so I doubt he had them," Husher answered.

"His wallet was on the counter in the apartment, his medication is still in the cabinet," Miss Moon continued for him.

"Okay, I have to ask, but was he feeling suicidal or having any mental health issues? Basically, do you think he is in any danger of hurting himself?"

Husher *almost* laughed.

He managed a shred of composure but wasn't sure how. Jared was far from the perfect image of mental health. He had to deal with a lot from a young age. Having the people meant to love him see him only as an inconvenience was not something anyone would take well. However, Jared had been doing better. He was done with high school and getting ready to go to a town over for college like most of their friend group, Husher and Mason were at least, Lee was the only one who had to deal with their senior year alone.

Jared was not the same kid he used to be and he was making roots in the town whether he knew it or not. He was a plant dad if nothing else, he would not just up and leave after all the time he spent taking care of all the plants he had in his room and in his and Miss Moon's apartment.

Samuel at least knew them, he knew that Miss Moon had legally taken Jared in when he was sixteen—technically it wasn't a legal adoption until seventeen, but the sheriff at the time was willing to overlook it given the lengthy run-ins the Baylor family seemed to have. Getting Jared out of there took priority. One of the perks of living in a small town Husher supposed, if you knew the right people, things could work out in your favor.

Husher let Miss Moon do most of the talking, telling the sheriff about how they tried calling Jared, how they asked around for any clues or hints as to where Jared might have gone. Talking with regular customers and friends Jared interacted with, even looking online for answers. Jared did little with social media, having a private account and forgetting it existed half the time. His last post was the first of September telling Lee happy birthday with pictures of them over the last year.

They finished up by giving his description. Most of which Samuel already knew.

"He turned eighteen on the fourteenth of June?"

"Yes," Miss Moon answered.

"Couldn't forget a fellow Gemini," Samuel typed out his answers, informing them what he was writing and giving them room to change it or correct him on any of it.

"He's five-foot-five-inches, compact build, Caucasian, cis male, a crescent moon behind his ear—"

"Left ear, and a nostril piercing on the same side," Husher filled in.

"Got it," Samuel nodded. "He was last seen wearing black jeans, a black hoodie, gray flannel, and red Converse sneakers."

They both nodded.

"And off the record," Samuel looked at Miss Moon, "you tried magic?"

"There is something blocking the location spell. It happens from time to time, but I haven't been able to get anywhere with it."

"Well, most missing persons turn up within that twenty-four-hour mark but the forty-eight hour mark is just as important. There is still time. If not, I will send for a search party. He might have just wandered in the woods, and while I know everyone here knows their way around, it was dark out when he was last seen. He could have easily just gotten lost and wandered too far."

Husher only nodded in response. He knew that could have been a possibility. Husher knew Jared could see in the dark, but it wasn't the same clear monochromatic view Husher had with his wolf eyes, it still left Jared with only a slight advantage of not being totally in the dark.

"I will let you know when we find anything of importance, but I'm afraid there isn't much we can do. He is low risk and an adult, unfortunately. While it might not be normal behavior, people aren't always who we think they are," Samuel said gently.

Husher knew the sheriff most likely had to say those things, to inform them that anything was possible, but Husher didn't have to believe it. He knew Jared down to the deodorant the man wore, they had no secrets... at least to Husher they didn't. The longer this went on the less sure he was about how well he knew his best friend.

Over the next few days, Husher felt like he was just going through the motions the more he looked into things.

After filing the report, the sheriff organized a search party the next day. People from the town joined in along with a few volunteers from neighboring towns. Mason, Lee, and their families all joined as well. They walked down paths in the woods that surrounded Lones Lake. Paths they all had grown up on and knew like the back of their hands. Summers spent outside until it was dark, winters where they had snowball fights, and autumn and springs where the weather was just right to go for a hike.

"I feel like we should have found something already," Mason muttered.

The tall trees around them were something Husher normally found comforting, but now it felt like they were looming over him, closing in on him with each step. It had been a good two hours of walking with only some muddy shoes to show for it. Listening to the people around him talk amongst themselves, chattering about nothing Husher cared to pay attention to.

"If there is something out here, we will find it," Jason, Mason's dad, told them. "It's not like a scent will just disappear in such a short time frame."

Husher knew that was true, then again as he breathed in the crisp September air—cold enough for hoodies, the humidity from summer washed away, he smelled nothing. Only the scents of those around him. Husher was close enough to Jared to know his scent, just like he knew Mason's and Lee's. Just like he knew his parents and Ava's.

Yet, it was no use in finding out where Jared Baylor was.

The cherry on the sundae was when he managed to find Joel in a small group a little ways in front of them. He nearly slowed his pace just to avoid the man. Husher didn't need to hear the deputy's opinions. Yet, as he got closer he couldn't help but listen to them anyway.

"Who's to say he wasn't like his parents, you know," Joel muttered. He wasn't too far ahead of them, talking to one of the bartenders from the local—and only—bar in town.

"Nah, he's a good kid." Mr. Harrison muttered. "He was the one to bring a pie when Marlen passed her nursing exam."

Joel just shook his head.

Husher glared when he looked back over to them. It wasn't the first time he wondered if he ran fast enough if he could smack the smug, shit-eating grin off the deputy's face.

"Still, he might have been smarter about hiding it. You think Brian was always a sack of shit. Hell, Karen was the class president freshman year," Joel continued, unable to read the energy around him.

"Don't," Lee muttered.

Husher bit back his comment and Mason seemed to know what he was thinking—no doubt thinking it too. Joel knew just as much as anyone the Baylors were *not* mentioned. While Jared was used to the comments—used to people thinking he was a deadbeat or only nice to get something out of it—Husher, Mason, and Lee all were quick to tell whoever it was off.

"You know he probably just fucked off and got high or maybe he started seeing shit like his mother—"

Husher rushed forward, fully done caring about the actions and consequences of punching a police officer. He brought his arm back only to be dragged back with it by rough hands. Mason and her dad were quick to rush forward after him. Jason pulled him back by one arm and Mason tugged on his other arm in a death grip.

Joel turned back, his cocky grin plastered on his pasty white face. "Do it, see how well it works out for ya."

Husher took a breath.

He wouldn't get anywhere if he did something. But damn if his wolf wasn't screaming at him, seeing red as he took another breath.

He let himself be pulled back.

Jason and Mason put him between his parents as if his wolf was still a pup learning just how quickly he could get angry. Husher focused on his task at hand. Finding a scent and not listening to the people around him. And when that didn't work, he sunk his claws into the palms of his hands every time he wanted to punch Joel. He just hoped they would scab over before anyone noticed.

They spent hours in the woods. It was cold, and near the two-hour mark it started raining. Just like the people's mood swings, the weather in Pennsylvania could be unpredictable.

The day was a blur.

After hours in the cold only to come up with nothing, Miss Moon made everyone tea before heading back into the woods with Husher. There had to be something they weren't seeing. Something that would help them.

Yet, there was nothing.

Like everything around him, it was painfully the same.

MISSING

HAVE YOU SEEN THIS MAN?

JARED BAYLOR, BROWN HAIR, BROWN EYES,
18 YEARS OLD, CAUCASIAN, 5'5" (165 CM)
LAST SEEN IN LONES LAKE PA, ON 05, SEPTEMBER

INFORMATION NEEDED
(XXX)-XXX-XXXX

Chapter Five
You Need to Shut Up

Jared Baylor – 06, October (Friday)

It had been a month, a full thirty-one days and counting. Upstairs in the extra room he dragged the pencil down and created another tally mark on the wall near the window. He didn't know how long he would keep it up. Each day blurred to the next, and with his sleep schedule, he wasn't all that sure his numbers were even right.

Within the first month there, he knew fighting back would be an overall lost cause. He was never good at fighting back, having the coordination of an inflatable air dancer found in an abandoned car dealership. While the Graham family might not have been overly strong they were unpredictable as ever, which was almost worse.

He had a suspicion Brandy was a witch or had seriously pissed off a ghost or two in the past to leave the house as haunted—or cursed—as it was. The few times he was able to get to a door, it was blocked off. He could see them walk out of it normally, but when he tried it was like an invisible barrier was in his way. It pulled him back in, as if the house was alive. While Jared knew supernatural creatures existed—he was living proof—he also knew the house itself was not the cause for it. Working with Miss Moon as much as he did he suspected there was some kind of magic involved.

Instead, Jared found hiding spots. Several not being ideal, like how he had to hold his nose for a while if he went out to the garage to sit, the smell of something burning had yet to fade into numbness and he cringed every time he breathed.

Dealing with all the unpleasantries was better than the alternative of running into the family. He knew he was shit at fighting, but that didn't mean he could try his best to avoid everyone.

Jordan was already downstairs, the fact the man was even alive was a red flag of its own. Watching him talk to himself was the cherry on top of it all.

When he turned and noticed Jared, he grinned.

"You know you're going to have to start pulling your weight. We can't do everything for you."

Jared wanted to laugh. He needed to be doing things for these people now?! He'd rather cover himself in pollen and see how minor his allergy actually was than to help the people who were actively keeping him from leaving.

Jared settled on saying a simple, "go fuck yourself."

It didn't take long for him to realize how much he had fucked up. Jordan rushed toward him, surprisingly quick for someone who was as malnourished as he was. Jared ran up the stairs not waiting to see what happened if he was caught. He was three steps away from being safe when Jordan grabbed him by the ankle and dragged him the rest of the way down. Jared hit his head but didn't feel dizzy. He blinked. His vision was clear, so it was unlikely he had a concussion—or at least he hoped he didn't. Jared tried to get free, but kicking at Jordan only did so much as he was dragged into the kitchen.

"Aw come on," Jordan grinned. "A bloodsucker like you can do better than that."

So he wanted Jared to fight him? Jared genuinely didn't understand what the hell was going on nor did he actually care to put the effort into something he knew would be worse for him in the end. There was no promise that if he killed any of them it would get him out of there. Just because he had to drink blood every few months to stay alive didn't mean he had any less morals when it came to murder.

"Why would I bother?" Jared muttered. "Looks like time will take care of that for me."

Jordan scrunched up his face, irritated as usual. He would probably end up with frown lines that constantly looked like he was constipated or had found a bug in his food.

Jared did his best to get up, but it ended up with him being punched in the face. Maybe not commenting would work out better for him in the future.

Jordan grumbled something Jared was too annoyed to listen to. The pasty dude spit on the ground and laughed as if it were the most entertaining thing he'd seen all day... which to be fair it probably was.

"Don't get in my way again, bloodsucker."

Jared was used to comments, and while 'bloodsucker' was more derogatory than anything else, it was also the most common. They could at least come up with something more clever at this point.

He lay there for a moment listening to the sound of the door opening and closing. When he knew Jordan was out of the house and most likely not coming back for several hours, Jared finally got up.

He walked out to the garage this time. The mess of the house made for some of the easier hiding spots, the garage especially. When he noticed that none of the family used that space all that much, it made it even more appealing. There were a few times Terry walked out there to grab something for the garden, but he would always disappear quickly. Jared never questioned it more than that.

Jared climbed up to a storage area where he had just enough room to move around but not enough to stand up. Moving a plastic storage bin, he hid behind it and covered himself with one of the blankets Cheryl and he had found while looking through the basement.

When it came to treating any wounds he was limited to the weeds Granny brought in from the backyard. It wasn't always helpful, but her ironically helping him was a bit amusing given his current situation. While he wasn't able to venture outside, he picked through the random weeds she assumed were plants.

Jared knew Granny was the one who had pulled him back the last time he got a little too close to the door. The pain in his arm as her long pointy nails had dug in; whether it was on purpose or not Jared didn't care to think about it again.

Finding weeds to help keep from infections was easy since he helped Moon collect things for the diner or for her spells. There were many late nights of collecting the correct things, cleansing them with moon water and/or storing them properly. Common plantain was one weed that was rather abundant in the backyards. Even with where they were, the backyard wasn't quite as bad as Jared would expect from seeing the rest of the house. It was overgrown and given the weather most of the plants were dead, but Granny seemed to take care of most of it. Jared assumed it was one of her delusions—constantly working on something out there.

It was just difficult getting into her stash when she came back into the house. Jared had to wait in the kitchen and pretend to help her. Something he failed at most of the time, but the few times he was able to get a handful of the random things she collected outside without being noticed were mostly worth it—luckily enough, Jared was able to recognize the common yard weed a handful of times. It was something small that helped but it was better than nothing. He remembered from a report he did at one time. The plant was rather distinct, dark green with an oblong kind-of shape, little veins running down the surface of the leaves. He mostly used it for helping heal any wounds along the way and to bring down any inflammation. He used it for the countless bug bites he got there. Jared was pretty sure he had seen more bugs inside the house than he ever had outside.

He just crushed the leaves and put them in the area that felt the worst. However, it wouldn't do much for the bruise that would be on his nose by the end of the day most likely. Not drinking anything along with not even consuming human food, his healing abilities weren't working like they usually did.

The garage seemed to be the one place he could think.

One of the few times he knew he wouldn't be found.

He was able to give in to the self-isolation that liked to kick him to the ground. He was able to *try* and cope enough to work on his plan of getting out of there.

The Graham house had no running water, no working electricity. Jared had learned early on that he didn't have his phone when he woke up. He hoped he lost it somewhere out in the woods and that the family didn't take it. He didn't think he could deal with having a way to call for help be so close. It took more to deal with that than the fact he was being stuck with a family out of a murder mystery novel. Like his own personal supernatural hunters who instead of killing him quickly were letting him waste away in a slow and annoying death.

Jared wished he had his phone.

He had pictures of his room at the diner, a place Moon invited him in and that he had called home. He had pictures of the food Moon made on the weekends, testing out the specials for the week. He had pictures of his friends being idiots, no one having the same facial expression in any image. Pictures of Husher being moody because Rooty and even Marco liked Jared more. Jared thought about the times he stayed over at Husher's and how when he went for a walk with Husher, Rooty, and Marco; his three blond boys who would all get equally as excited about walk time.

He hated the thought of losing the pictures of them, eventually even losing old memories. Having to come to terms with losing his acceptance letter for the local college. He remembered taking a picture with it, a thumbs up and a stupid grin on his face that he would definitely think was awkward later but at the time he was too excited to really care. He had planned to frame it, partially because he thought it would be funny but also because it meant he actually was working on completing something he never thought he would get to do.

Something that without actual proof he would have never believed to be real life.

Now in a cold garage, up where boxes of old clear string lights sat, he was collecting as much dust as them. It wasn't fair, and too many times he got stuck with that thought. It never helped to think like that, but it didn't quite help him to stop.

The door to the garage opened and Jared held his breath, waiting for the person to leave so he could get back to his depressive train of thought where he was the captain *and* the passenger.

"You know, if you'd keep your comments to yourself he wouldn't keep picking on you," Cheryl murmured.

Jared breathed out a sigh of relief but otherwise didn't move. He knew she was right; he had tried to keep his comments to himself, but living with Moon gave him the confidence not to have to look over his shoulder anymore. To speak as freely as he wished.

He thought it, he fucking said it.

It was simple and problematic when it came to most of his interactions with people.

"I know," he grumbled.

She paused for a moment, so used to keeping her comments to herself that when she had the chance to say something she almost didn't know how to say it.

"Then why do it?" she finally asked.

Jared didn't want to say it was because he didn't know how to shut up. That he was friends with a werewolf and a banshee and he had to be loud or he would not be able to get his point across as effectively. Because he's an asshole who despite his inability to be anything else doesn't desire to feel like he can get away with anything.

"Anything broken?" Cheryl asked after not getting an answer.

Jared shook his head. Wincing at the feeling and also at how stupid it was since Cheryl couldn't see him from his hiding spot.

"No."

She seemed to accept his answer and let it go. She was fairly easy going, but a part of him never understood how someone could stay there that long. She seemed physically able to leave as far as he knew, but it felt like overstepping to asked why she stayed. The last thing he needed was to be on another person's shit list.

"I'll bring you something before dinner if you want to nap. We won't see them again until late at night. Saw Terry take a snack with him," Cheryl said as if she were reading the newspaper.

After staying there so long, she at least knew how to read the family and knew their schedules no matter how much they seemed to change to Jared. He stopped questioning it and left it alone. He didn't bother saying anything. He knew Cheryl was more or less just informing him about the situation than anything else. Soon enough, she left just as quickly as she appeared.

Jared relaxed the best he could into his makeshift bed and closed his eyes. He would eventually fall asleep.

The daylight hours always were a bit drowsy for him anyway, and it wasn't like he had anything else to do. He closed his eyes wishing it was all a hellish nightmare.

Chapter Six
Another Dead End

Husher Carden – 12, November (Sunday)

"You are not going and bothering them again?" Nicole said, a little irritated. "If they find something, trust me, you'll be the first to know."

Husher knew his mom wasn't being rude about it. He had gone to the police station or called weekly for any updates, yet sixty-seven days later Jared Baylor was still missing, and with each day it seemed like fewer and fewer people cared.

"That's what I told him," Mason muttered, half a blueberry muffin in her mouth.

"And I'm perfectly fine ignoring both of you," Husher deadpanned.

"Where did we go wrong with him?" Lee muttered to Husher's parents.

Dawn just chuckled before giving her son a sad look. Husher was tired of it all. He didn't need people looking at him like he was somehow in the wrong for wanting to find his best friend. He wasn't going to give up and chalk it up to Jared leaving without telling anyone just because he was eighteen and could—it didn't mean that's what he did.

"Husher, my dude," Mason started this time, chewing her food before talking. "I don't know why you need their help, you're more qualified at this point—also don't talk to me or your mom like that. We will expect an apology any time now."

"I think you mean accept," Lee muttered.

"Depends on the level of sincerity," Mason smiled.

Husher sighed. He obviously tried on his own to find Jared and he had no idea what to do or where else to look.

"Mom, I am sorry," Husher muttered sincerely and kissed her on the cheek before he sat down at the counter. "Mas, you'll get over it eventually."

"Bitch," Mason grumbled before finishing her muffin.

Husher smiled, unbothered by her comment as he ate his own breakfast. Lee would most likely give in and go with him to the authorities. It felt all too much like rock-bottom, even as it showed that Husher and his friends were not going to just let this be an unsolved case. Forgotten about until some white woman with a podcast and true crime addiction found out about it and solved it years too late.

"I'm just going to see if they have any updates," Husher sighed. "I really don't see what the big deal is."

When no one said anything—even Mason, who never shut up—Husher knew it was another one of those moments no one knew what to say to him. He pretended not to notice the silence and cleared his plate.

"I'll go with you," Lee muttered. "I promised donuts for Cody and Trinity," they explained.

Husher nodded and put his shoes on by the door before grabbing his keys. "I'll be back later. Ava, please don't get bribed into letting Mason move my room around again."

"No promises," Ava grinned.

Mason fist-bumped her. "I might even have a few of those mini plastic ducks left."

"Mama," Husher whined.

Dawn rolled her eyes at them, but he knew she would stop them from doing something stupid. His mom, on the other hand, would encourage all harmless chaotic behavior all day any day.

"I will handle it, go and don't be gone all day." Dawn swished her hand in the air gesturing for them to go already.

Lee was behind him as Husher walked out of his house, shutting the door behind them. Lee had their black fanny pack slung over their chest. Few things they wore lacked pins or patches, and while Husher had the most colorful aesthetic in their friend group, Lee had the most pins stuck to jackets or cardigans, or in this case, their fanny pack.

After a minute Lee was walking beside him Husher couldn't help but ask: "You'd tell me if I was searching for a lost cause here, right?"

Lee met his eyes for a moment. Their wavy brown hair was pulled half up, leaving the ends of electric blue a little less bold than it was when they had their hair down.

"I'd have to," Lee nodded.

As if it were really that simple. Husher left it at that and they walked the rest of the way in silence.

The police station was getting to be way too familiar for his liking. He walked up to the brick building where too many tax dollars were spent—given how small their town was. He took a breath before walking in and over to Samuel's secretary.

"Mr. Carden, didn't I tell you I'd have the sheriff himself call you if we got *any* updates?" Daloris muttered.

Husher nodded, used to feeling embarrassed about ignoring her comments by now. "I just thought since I was passing by that I would see if there was anything new."

Daloris shook her head. "Mm-hmm, well now you know we are not any closer than we were since yesterday."

He nodded and turned to leave. Lee opened the door and followed behind him to the diner. They had tried everything so far. They had tried tracking Jared's phone only to learn it must have died at some point leaving the records blank. Husher didn't know much more than how to use the basics of his phone. He often forgot how to change his wallpaper, and the few times he tried, he usually had to ask for help. However, Jared's phone being blank with no last location almost seemed like it was on purpose—almost as if someone turned it off. Husher and his friends had shared their locations in their group chat ever since they were freshmen in high school or since Mason unironically suggested it just in case they ever needed to know where someone in their group was.

The true-crime felt a little too *true* for Husher at the moment.

In the end, it had done nothing for them.

There was nothing they could do at this point. Mason and Lee went along with him walking around town—spots Jared liked to walk to—in hopes of finding something they had missed. Even trying to track his scent left them nowhere closer to finding him.

"We could look through his laptop again?" Lee offered.

They walked into the diner, and Lee stood in line to order their cousins' food. Husher thought about the offer. When they got the laptop back from the police they found nothing useful nor did Husher find anything out of the norm.

"You don't mind?" Husher asked.

"It gives me time to avoid Debra working in the living room and my grandma who keeps telling her off because she is trying to watch her show," Lee answered.

Husher nodded and wasted no time in heading up to the apartment. Miss Moon was used to him being there even when Jared wasn't missing. It was normal for Husher to wander up and into their apartment, bursting in as if it were a second home. It still felt weird walking into Jared's room when he wasn't there though. Husher ignored the pit in his stomach and grabbed the laptop before quickly leaving.

"I texted Mason, we can just go to her house," Lee informed him when he came back down to the diner. "Plus, she knows everyone's passwords anyway."

Husher nodded. While he forgot his own passwords the second he made them, Mason regularly changed hers and managed to be the password person with close friends and relatives.

The walk to Mason's house didn't take long. She lived the closest to town due to her and her father working at the same garage right in the middle of Lones Lake. Ironically, the Whites' house was stained black brick and looked more like something out of a gothic dream than anything else. Even in the summer when Mason's parents planted flowers in the front flower beds, they were filled with *blackberry petunias* since anything else would not go with the aesthetic. Husher was used to it by now; it would've been strange to see anything else there at this point. Though they did do a rainbow flower bed once for pride month to piss off the neighbors across the street, which was the right level of petty he knew Mason's parents to have.

They knocked on the door and Mason's dad, Jason, was the one to answer. He was five-foot-seven inches with all the charm of Mason—if she was nicer. To the smiley face he had tattooed on his middle finger just because he thought it would be funny, to the eyebrow piercings and his t-shirt collection, today being a cartoon seahorse in pastel blue, light pink and with a hint of white, he looked just as punk as the rest of his family. His dark brown hair was mostly covered by a hat, so on days like casual Sundays when he was off work it was often left an unstyled mess. He looked the most like Mason, with warm brown skin and brown eyes that always reminded Husher of the color of the pinecones he collected near winter.

Jason smiled at them and greeted them in Spanish, something Husher was pretty sure Lee only half understood, as they were let into the house. Mason was in the kitchen working on her actual breakfast with her siblings.

Jules was finishing up their food when Husher and Lee walked into the kitchen area that doubled as the dining room. Jules was the oldest by a year and always smelled like banana flavored bubble gum. They worked as a web designer and worked from home most of the time. Their short dark brown hair that was shaved with faded sides, taking more after Philip with the same level of casualness. Much like Lee, they were aro/ace and had the pride flag pins on their shirt to match.

"About time, I thought you two were never showing up," Mason muttered.

"We're ten minutes early," Lee stated.

Mason shook her head in dismissal as if they were the ones in the wrong. Husher knew Lee was always on time—if not early—for everything. However, they let it go and made themselves at home as Mason ate.

"You're sure you don't want anything?" Philip asked.

Philip White was a year younger than his husband, but more often than not it seemed to be the other way around when Husher talked to them. Philip was pretty casual about most things, and his shaved head made him look much tougher than he actually was.

It was almost impossible to find the werewolf intimidating when his favorite thing about winter was binge-watching Christmas movies in his themed pajamas with his family. He was slightly taller than Husher at six-foot-one, dark eyes to match his onyx septum ring.

"We just ate," Lee informed him.

"What about coffee?" Philip offered.

They both agreed.

"So you wanna look through his laptop again?" Mason asked.

"What if we missed something or if something was taken off of it recently?" Husher asked.

Mason nodded. "I mean what do we have to lose? Plus, having a reason to snoop through Jared's laptop is at least entertaining," Mason muttered. She was most likely just trying to lighten the mood but Husher and Lee couldn't help but agree.

Seeing all the saved fanfictions he had from *ao3* alone was enough of an answer, but seeing the color coded document filled and organized alphabetically by ship was a bit amusing to know how neat it was all logged onto his laptop... yet, his room always looked like a mini tornado ran through it.

"You just like being noisy," her little brother, Owen muttered. He walked out with Cuddles, the family snake, wrapped around his arm. He waved with his free arm before grabbing his drink and heading into the living room. Owen was the youngest at thirteen and he looked a lot like Mason. When he was a toddler he looked nearly identical to her baby pictures, and Husher would never get tired of teasing her about it.

By the time they made it to Mason's room, they had coffee in hand and a mini muffin made of eggs and filled with cheddar cheese.

Mason sat at her desk with the laptop, Lee on the fluffy rug, and Husher flopped back onto the bed much like Mason would do when she came over to his house.

Mason's room was surprisingly clean in an organized way only she understood. The forest green walls and black ceiling were the perfect fit for her style. She had mini mushroom-shaped string lights up along the ceiling that always looked nice when they had a group sleepover at her house. There were a few framed posters hung up on the walls, and a flag above her desk with shades of orange, white, and pink on it. It was one of the few colorful things in her room. The big rug that took up most of the floor was always even softer than it looked, which made for a good sensory toy for Jared and Lee everytime they stayed over.

"I don't know what we're going to find that we didn't before," she said.

Mason opened the laptop with a sigh and quickly signed in with the password she refused to let Husher *specifically* know. He didn't really know why now of all times she refused to tell him, but he let it go. He didn't truthfully need to know anyway... he was just a bit curious about it.

She clicked a few things, looking through all the recent documents first, and filtered through it all. Husher watched from his spot on the bed, looking over her shoulder to note there was nothing. She looked through his search history only to find a few horror story videos he listened to, abandoned houses, what the correct spelling of *spaghetti* was, along with his searches for the perfect fanfic that had something to do with lemons or something.

Nothing had changed since they last looked.

Part of him hoped there would have been a hint of something he hadn't seen before. Instead, he lost yet another argument to the people who claimed Jared ran away.

Husher knew better. Lee knew better. Hell, even Mason knew better.

They all knew Jared wouldn't have left right when his life was his own. Not when he was eighteen and legally able to live long-term with Miss Moon without having to worry about his biological parents dragging him into their bullshit time and time again.

"I mean, even the pigs visited the Baylors," Mason started as if sharing the same brainwave. "Karen is in jail again, so she had nothing to do with it, and Brian will most likely rat out whoever he has been staying with soon enough."

"Exactly, so it's another dead end," Husher grumbled.

Mason handed back the laptop before shrugging. "There isn't anything on there. It's going to be a waste."

Husher got up, not wanting to hear any of what Mason had bluntly informed him of, but ultimately he knew that would be the case. They checked before and there was nothing useful. *Why would this time be any different?*

Lee left with him, but once in the town square, they went their separate ways. Husher walked home only to flop on the couch with his mama, who was reading. She

combed her fingers through his blond hair but said nothing, which he was grateful for.

He had to figure this out.

He was *not* going to lose his best friend... for good.

Chapter Seven
Eat Your Dinner, Boy

Jared Baylor – 21, November (Tuesday)

"Well, that's promising," Jared muttered to himself. It was just about as promising as talking to himself was. It seemed to be one of the only ways he could pass the time or get through a day without slipping into a mindset he didn't want to slip into again.

Feeling guilty over his years of depression—even if he wasn't sure why he felt guilty about it in the first place—when things were supposed to be getting better it only made the guilt worse. It wasn't eating away at him anymore, at least at the moment. What chewed at him now was the fact that he was trapped in a house that felt more like a game of survival than anything else.

It just seemed like the whole day was as promising as his stay with the Graham family—as promising as the day already was—which meant nothing.

Jared knew too much about them to be able to leave now, even if the bag of bones currently humming songs in the kitchen would let him. None of his knowledge could help him understand why they took him in the first place.

Was it personal?

Did he do something wrong to someone and not know it? Maybe he sleepwalked. Maybe they knew his bio parents and they didn't pay them, so they were using him as leverage to get what they wanted.

He genuinely hoped that wasn't the reason. He would be stuck with the Graham family until he died if that was the case.

Was it random?

Was he just in the wrong place at the wrong time, walking too close to their house and they saw him as a threat? Him trespassing on their property and just not knowing it?

Or was it because he's a vampire?

People had gotten used to the supernatural people coming out, living among them since the dawn of time and finally getting recognized by governments of nearly every country—some with better rights than others. It was nothing new, vampires and other supernatural people had been known since Jared could remember, but hunters still existed, and groups trying to kill them were few to little but still a real threat in some places. And mixed families like Jared's bio parents were even more of a target. Having a human and vampire reproduce was not something people took too well.

At the end of the day, Jared had no idea what it even was. All he knew was that he was fucking over it. Hiding in the garage knowing that it was going to be a shitty day was not something he was happy about. Ignoring the hunger pains and the constant need for water was a full-time job. He could only get up for water. Water that was even worse than what he had to drink from the river while on a camping trip through filtered straws that Husher lost on the second day.

"I might have dropped mine, so I took yours... then dropped it into the creek too," Husher had muttered, scratching the back of his neck out of nervous habit. Leaving Mason and Lee the only ones who offered the extras they had.

He would have killed to have been back to that moment than in the five-star hell hole that was the Graham family house.

Jared heard Granny working in the kitchen all morning. She had been cooking all day, which was never a good thing, and they all knew it. Dinner was always a brownish mush that made him want to vomit at the sight alone. It was like something now burned deep into his mind, he could smell it just by thinking about it.

At this point he'd settle on being able to go out into the garden behind the house and eat something out there. Even with the winter season approaching, leaving the plants and even the stubborn weeds dead or dying.

When Jared hid in the garage again it was only a blatant reminder that the weather outside was going to make things so much worse for him. He didn't have to look outside to know that it was cold and rainy, and while rainy weather was usually a good thing for him, he currently felt too much like a lizard who accidentally traveled to Canada in the middle of winter. Jared needed the sun, just enough so he could recharge without being sick; enough so he could move his limbs without feeling like someone put him in slow motion. Though today he felt like it just added to the uncomfortable homesick feeling that lived like a constant bug in his head. He dreadfully hoped it wasn't an actual bug. It wouldn't be all that shocking to him if something crawled into his ear while he slept.

He opened his eyes at the thought. Yep, he was definitely not getting any sleep.

He felt cold constantly and having next to zero energy made it difficult to even sleep the day away. He had no plan, no energy, and no idea how he could even manage such a task at this point.

"Just another day," he tried to convince himself.

It never worked. Telling himself to get through just another day was about as helpful as colored pencils were to someone who had achromatopsia and could only see in black, white, or shades of gray. He knew he needed to grasp some kind of hope. Even the maladaptive daydreaming felt like he was trying too hard to feel something—anything that wasn't screaming to him about the hopelessness of it all. The overall lack of information on how or why he was even stuck there, to begin with, was annoying. How the hell did he manage to get stuck in a house that rivaled any horror movie he had ever seen? Of course, the only logical answer would have been that he was dead somehow and this was his own personal Hell... or maybe he died in the house and now he was forced to haunt the place and the Graham family were all ghosts too.

Every time he had the thought it only made him have more questions that led him down paths he wanted nothing to do with. He didn't need to be thinking that way, but it wasn't like it was impossible. He could have been seeing things the whole time; he didn't know what was real anymore.

He lay back, the makeshift bed still just as uncomfortable as it was since the day he found the space. Jared closed his eyes and willed his mind to keep the disturbing dreams to themselves. He needed to sleep, but it felt like damnation closing his eyes and giving in.

When Jared woke up he truly wished he hadn't. He wasn't sure if he meant at all or if he wished he hadn't gone to sleep in the first place but waking up to a nightmare of its own was not pleasant.

Being dragged to the dinner table—and if the moldy socks were anything to take note of, it was Jordan throwing him into his chair this time.

"About time, boy," Terry snapped.

Jared looked around the table.

Cheryl was already there, sitting next to Sabrina as usual. Granny at the head of the table, her daughter-in-law and son closest to her. Jordan was at the end of the table and staring distantly at it—a bug crawling off the edge and onto Terry's lap was gross but not surprising.

The warm plate put in front of him was worse.

"No one is leaving the table until y'all eat up. I didn't cook this to look at it," Granny hissed.

Jared never met either set of grandparents. Relatives were one of the topics his bio parents refused to talk about. So that left Lee's grandmother the only thing close to a grandparent that he knew. Shirley Cleamon was nothing like the hag he was forced to sit at a table with currently. Jared took a fake bite knowing he would need to get out of there before time was up. There was no way he would be able to finish any of it. Even as he faked a bite, there was only so much he could throw onto the floor.

"A fat boy like you would eat a lot more than that!" Terry shouted.

Of course, he would fucking notice.

Over the weeks he had been there Jared had lost a fair amount of weight, enough to use a makeshift belt on his pants to keep them up. Though he was used to ignoring comments about his body, growing up with his classmates who loved to call him the runt of the litter—even if he was *thankfully* an only child—the comments still made little sense to him.

"Eat the damn dinner," Granny ordered.

Brandy looked over at him. "I mean look at the plate. He isn't even touching it!"

"So ungrateful," Jordan commented.

"Eat your damn supper!" Terry demanded.

Jared tried faking taking another bite to get them to ignore him. He grabbed the spoon, ignored the grime on it, and held his breath as he faked the bite.

Jordan threw his spoon at him and grinned as he went to call him out for the trick. Jared glared and took a bite, regretting it immediately. The texture was like wet cardboard mashed together. Then the taste kicked in, making him sick immediately. Moldy food with bugs taking residency in it would have been superior to the hot garage he had just eaten. He still felt like he was going to be sick. He couldn't swallow it, he knew that if he did he would throw it up but if he spit it out in front of Granny he didn't know what punishment he would get.

His hands shook, a cool sweat already covering his body. He forced himself to swallow the bite of food. Holding his breath for a moment afterwards in an attempt to not throw up. He couldn't eat human food after so long without blood. It made him sick every time. Though he wasn't sure if that was the reason or if it was because the term *food* was so loosely used for the mush in front of him.

"It's very good tonight, Granny," Cheryl tried to help.

It was no use. Granny had snapped, slamming her hands down on the table as if she was trying to break it. It took seconds for Terry to take that moment and stand up, his chair skidding back and crashing to the ground. He rushed forward and over to Jared only to raise his hand and cruelly slap him across the face.

"Oh, so my cooking ain't good enough for you huh?!" Granny screeched.

And really he wanted to yell that, *yes*, it absolutely was *that* bad. He had no idea how any of them were still alive at this point. Even with the rations that had been delivered by someone who knew they had taken Cheryl and Jared. He couldn't help but want to see them rot along with the family in front of him.

Terry slapped him again. "She's talkin' to you, boy!"

His ear was ringing; he felt detached from his body and unable to talk. Almost like a full system shutdown. His mind taking over and actively ignoring everything around him.

Jared was only able to watch what was happening around him—what was happening to him. It felt like he was seeing it from someone else's point of view, unable to process anything at all.

He had no idea how to get control again.

He felt like he couldn't so much as move his arm to punch the bastard back. He was just as useless as he was when he was a kid. He was over the helpless feeling; he was so tired of feeling like that. Feeling—knowing—there was nothing he could do to help himself get out of there. He didn't even have control of his own body at the moment. He just let each punch land again and again, apparently choosing to deal with the pain that would hit him later. His head felt like it was underwater, and he knew he was being screamed at. He knew the vein in Terry's neck would only make him sick if he bit it—ripped it from his body and let the man bleed out as he became the feral vampire the sick monster hunters liked to think he was.

In reality, he was sinking lower and lower.

It was the moment he *knew* he would die there. The thought was almost welcoming. Being able to end it all would be better than dealing with them. Having to be pushed back into old trauma responses he thought he had grown out of. Feeling the same shit now as he had then.

It wasn't right.

He got out of there.

Why did he have to fight again to get out of a place with another careless family?!

How was that fair?!

Jared felt his head go numb with the rest of his body. He would no doubt have a problem tending to the damage later, but there was nothing he could really do. He forced his eyes closed, willing his body to pass out already, to let the world fade to a pretty black.

The world around him was nothing; *he* was nothing.

After all, he knew better than to think *he* would get a happy ending.

Chapter Eight
Blog Posts and Twin Daggers

Husher Carden – 27, November (Monday)

At first, Husher had no idea why he woke up. His eyes blurred as he looked around his dark room, the only light coming from the color-changing moon he had on his desk. Everything seemed normal enough, so he laid his head back down.

Before he could fall asleep again his phone rang. The buzz was enough to startle him, and the fact it was the middle of the night definitely made him bolt up at the sound.

Quickly he sat and scrambled to reach for his phone while simultaneously swiping to answer it before checking to see who it even was. Clearly it was important—calling twice in the middle of the night was never *good* news.

"Hello?!" Husher panicked as he put the phone up to his ear.

"Hey, sorry I woke you," Lee said, their voice too calm and smooth for the hour. "I was looking through old messages and found something."

It took Husher a minute to process where he was and what year it even was. He could have probably forgotten his own name at that moment. He took a minute and listened to Lee. Husher always liked how Lee spoke, right to the point and without much sugar coating. However, the long pauses and cliffhangers he could do without.

"You did not just call me in the middle of the night to tell me that and leave me to question what you found?!" Husher did his best to keep his voice down, not wanting to wake the rest of his house.

"It's actually morning by now, but no. I just thought you'd want to know."

For a long moment, Husher thought Lee was going to leave it there and just hang up, but they continued.

"It might be a long shot, but Jared was talking about the Paranoid House," Lee began. "It was the one all the freshmen were dared to go to at one point. No one was able to find it, so it just became another town rumor to scare kids."

Husher was confused because he was pretty sure he would have remembered something like that. If he could manage to remember the rumors it had something to do with being in bed before midnight on Halloween night or else the unknown creature would wake him up with all his toes eaten off or something. Then again if that was the case he was pretty sure he should have remembered what Lee was talking about.

Then he remembered one of the nights Jared had stayed over. They were freshmen at the time, and Lee and Mason had bailed because it was snowing too bad for anyone to drive—and walking in the weather would not be worth it. They were laying on the floor in a mass of pillows and blankets Jared had arranged perfectly for the movie night they prepared for. Though after two movies, they ended up watching horror stories on Husher's laptop instead.

Husher had looked up when the video mentioned their state, only a few hours in on their binge-watch. He remembered next to nothing other than staying up all night and eventually crashing sometime in the morning when the sun came up, deeming it safe enough to sleep. He didn't remember Jared mentioning the house after that. They looked into a few conspiracy blogs about it, but given that it was more a school rumor, it wasn't taken all that seriously.

"Make any connections?" Lee asked.

Husher remembered he was still on the phone and nodded, then remembered Lee couldn't see him. He seriously needed to stop doing that.

"Yeah. We read a few blog posts about it, but he never talked about it much more than that. Why would it have anything to do with him missing?"

Lee was silent again, and for a moment Husher thought they would make a good therapist. Long silences that made him want to talk to get rid of the uneasiness he felt with each second his ears rang from the silence.

"Meet me at the park," Lee finally replied. "I texted Mason to meet us there as well. I will explain then."

With that, Lee hung up.

Husher looked at his phone for a moment, long enough for the screen to fade to black and auto-lock. Jared wouldn't have gone looking for the house. *Not on his own, right?*

He got up, quietly changing into a gray hoodie and the same jeans he wore yesterday before making his way out of his room. He grabbed his shoes and disarmed the alarm before opening the door and getting out before his dogs heard him. He would have to remember to reset the alarm when he got back.

Husher remembered walking to the park a lot in the summer season. He and his friends would go out when it was dark enough to see any stars or whatever moon phases Jared needed to see. They would stay up listening to podcasts and horror channels while they sat at the playground in the middle of the night. Most of the stories were true but a few fan-made, and fictional ones were added to their watch lists. It was something that combined with the frogs and crickets that were perfectly loud and vocal during the summer season. It was a comforting feeling he never got over since.

Husher made his way to the playground, ignoring any hope of trying to get through to him. He didn't want to think about it until he heard Lee's theory. He did not need to overthink anything before he knew all the information.

Mason was on the swings when he got there.

He was going to ask if she remembered the rumors of the house, but Lee was running to get there, so it must have been imperative since they never ran if they could help it.

Husher looked over expectantly at them, too nervous to swing or do anything other than fidget in the spot he was standing in.

"So why couldn't you just tell me this over the phone?" Mason asked.

She kicked a bit of the dirt and wood chips up as she casually pushed back on the swing.

"Setting is key," Lee breathed out, sarcastically.

Mason looked over to Husher, sharing a glance that could only mirror the other in a *'what the fuck are they talking about this time?'* moment.

If Lee noticed, they ignored it instead pulling out their phone and scrolling through a few things before putting it back into their pocket.

"They could be tracking it all."

Mason sighed.

"Who?" Husher questioned.

"I don't know, to be honest. I just needed to go for a walk, and falling down a horror-filled rabbit hole is not the best when walking at night alone," Lee informed them.

"So we're here because you didn't want to be alone?" Mason deadpanned.

"I mean kinda—just shut up." Lee took a seat at one of the swings, pushing back with their feet. "I think I found something worth looking into."

Lee grabbed their phone again, this time clicking through their notes most likely. If Lee Cleamon was one thing, they were prepared for whatever topic they were going to be talking about.

"The Graham family lived off the grid," Lee started. "They had one kid, and from my understanding, that was around the time they needed to move. So they built the house known as a few different things over the years, but '*Paranoid House*' was what it was referred to the most."

Husher sat on the edge of the slide, ignoring the wood chips that would no doubt stick to his pants even after he washed them.

"So they were paranoid?" Mason asked. "Or the house made them that way?"

"Both?" Lee replied, though it sounded more like a question than anything else. "The dad took his wife and son to live in a house close to their small town. They seemed like a messy family based on the reports I looked into. Child abuse, neglect, the whole run of it all—so they could have just moved because of those claims."

"So basically they did nothing about the claims?" Husher asked, already knowing the answer.

Lee shook their head. "Not that I know of. It seems like it was the dad who had the paranoia and pushed it onto his wife who over the years got just as bad as he did. The son moved out for several years and started a family, but came back when his dad died and his mom needed him. I think this was where she brainwashed the son again, his wife, and two kids. Eventually, keeping them there, feeding them lies, and the more time they were isolated and cut off from reality, the more they believed it was the right thing to do."

"And you found this all through messages... how?" Mason questioned.

Husher sat back on the slide while he listened. He looked up at the sky and the stars that were welcomed by it and pushed down whatever worries he had until Lee was done talking. He promised himself that only then he could freak out.

"I found this through a missing persons case on Cheryl Wards, a sixteen-year-old who was last known to be going out to babysit for the Graham family. She has been missing for five years so far and no one has been able to find her. Some people believe they killed her when she went to work one night and never returned."

"And none of this was looked into?" Mason questioned.

"Public records said that a detective questioned the Graham family but they were never charged for anything," Lee answered. "The only thing about Cheryl I could find was that she was recently emancipated before she went missing."

Husher sat up. "How is any of this a good thing?!"

Lee pulled a paper out of their pocket. "Because I have the map for the house at least, which I found through Debra's real estate files while she was yelling at her brother for being an idiot."

Knowing how Lee's aunt and uncle fought it was most likely just the twins being idiots, but at least Debra refused to have any spawns so the cycle didn't have to continue—unlike Brett, who had two children.

"You have a map?!" Mason yelled in shock. "How?"

"Dude, look it up. Past real estate said it was sold back to the Graham family after financial issues in 2003." Lee shrugged. "So who's going with me?"

Husher stood up, dumbfounded. "Now?"

Lee nodded. "Well, it would be the easiest. If we find it now, the dark will help us hide."

"I have daggers!" Mason cheered.

Husher took a step back. "I don't feel comforted by that."

Mason blinked at him and shrugged, swinging back and forth. "You have claws, I don't feel comfortable about that."

"Yeah, but I'm not going to stab someone with them," Husher deadpanned.

"Name *one* person I stabbed," Mason demanded.

Lee raised their hand. "If it helps, I have a sword."

Husher sighed. "We will talk about why you two just casually have those weapons later," he muttered. "If it's worth giving it a shot, fine. I'll go."

"Okay, bitches—let's go then." Mason got up and started walking away before Lee stopped her.

"Pack a small backpack, water, a first aid kit, and a flashlight," Lee instructed. "We can meet back here when we're done and leave through the woods here, it should be the quickest route."

Husher couldn't help but look behind him, the wooded area covered in inky darkness; his imagination taking over and creating different shapes in the shadows.

"Okay, let's do it."

Husher could not believe he agreed to such a ridiculous plan or that Lee had been the one to come up with it. Yet, there he was trying to convince himself it was a good idea as he walked home and crept to his room, grabbing his backpack. He didn't bother worrying about the mess as he emptied it out onto his bed. He got the things he would need and quickly changed his shoes for ones better in mud.

When Husher walked out to the kitchen, he paused. He didn't want his parents to worry about him, so he looked through the junk drawer and grabbed a pen and paper. He wrote a simple note, leaving the location, the time, and the date, before he left.

He met his friends back outside at the park. Mason grinned as she flipped her twin daggers and Lee looked the same, just with their hair pulled back.

Mason flipped Husher off as soon as she saw him—for what reason, Husher didn't know—but he was used to it by now.

"Are we going to go kick some little bitches' asses?" Mason asked a bit too loudly for the hour.

"*We* aren't, but you're free to kick enough ass for all of us," Husher informed her.

Lee nodded in agreement.

Husher didn't know what he would find if anything at all, but it was worth a shot to look into. The house in question being so close formed a pit in Husher's stomach. If Jared was that close the whole time? He didn't want to believe it. If that was true they had been overlooking something so close.

Jared would have been stuck out there the entire time.

All the what if's that strangled his brain were worse than thinking he just ran away. At least if he ran away it could have been better than being stuck in an abandoned house with such a gruesome history.

"Stop thinking so damn much, dude." Mason bumped Husher's shoulder. "We are clearly professionals here. We have nothing to worry about," she muttered sarcastically.

Husher nodded, not actually believing it but going along with it anyway. They had a lot to worry about, and he knew it.

Chapter Nine
Frog Knick-Knacks

Jared Baylor – 27, November (Monday)

Freezing cold while staring out an open window was not the worst way to rot away.

Granted, Jared knew it wouldn't kill him, it would just slightly discomfort him sitting upstairs and in one of the junk rooms he had cleared his way to the window that overlooked the side yard. The cool wind of November sent chills down his spine. He knew he normally ran a bit colder than humans or werewolves, but the weather nearly had him second guessing if looking at the sky was worth his hands and feet going numb. Finding comfort in the darkness the night brought was something Jared was used to. Vampires might not have been known for walking around much in the sunlight but rather for hunting in the dead of night.

In reality, Jared just liked the calm the nighttime brought him.

The sounds of crickets, cicadas, amphibians, and anything that sang in the quiet air. It was something that changed with the seasons, summer being the loudest while winter was left with rustling leaves, or the howls of the wind blowing. However, along with the sounds, seeing the stars and learning their meanings, and learning which phase the moon was in were equally calming to him.

Jared looked up to the moon. At home he had made a chart for all the phases, taking note of all the full moons and what they meant. It started out as a hobby to distract him then turned into something he was actually interested in learning about.

He remembered how it always pissed Husher off that he knew so much about the moon phases—something that was not so easy for the blond to learn. Like the nights he would try and teach him but it seemed to go nowhere.

"I barely know what moon phase it is," Husher com-
plained.

Jared knew his best friend well enough to note Husher only
knew it was a full moon when he couldn't place why he felt
so weird, and even then someone had to inform him of the
date.

"You've brought shame to the werewolf community."
He clutched his non-existent pearls. "Rude!"
Jared couldn't help but laugh.

This night, however, looking out the open window in
the dead of night was not as calming as Jared would have
hoped it would be.

He watched the bright moon, a Gemini moon to be
exact. Something he remembered about manifesting the
need for changes and being spontaneous or something
like that came to mind. A time for thinking about his
feelings and sharing them with others and blah blah blah.
He didn't really think anything of it, never did, and being
stuck in a house of nightmares didn't put him in the mood
to be optimistic about it. So, he just took the facts he knew
and left it at that.

The rest of the sky was fairly dark; most of the stars
weren't visible with his limited view. He looked past the
mangled screen screwed into the window, noticing that

whoever installed it had apparently ignored the stainless steel latches on the sides completely.

He didn't know what to do with most of his time. Sitting in silence was a recurring nightmare for him. It left him time to think about memories he had, most of which seemed to be more bad than good. The past few days he had been stuck in a downward spiral of substandard and unwelcome memories left on repeat in his head.

Trips to town where he was on display as if vampires were not something that had been known and living among them for centuries. Jared was used to it, but it didn't mean it hurt any less. He knew he could never slip up, he knew he was always set on perfect behavior, and even then it was still an issue for some people.

Jared had long gotten used to the names they called him, the looks he got even if he did his best to clean up. He was used to the glares. Whispers about his family or of him being constantly dirty even if he used the gym showers or when Husher's moms let him stay over—which was more nights than not, so he just showered there.

Yet, the comments about his bio family being damned from the start, cursed genetics or just plain stupidity.

The rumors never stopped—the watchful eyes when he went into a store even if he had never stolen anything a day in his life, classmates who teased him constantly for being so short, or how when stood next to Husher, he was especially short in comparison.

He felt like he did then.

Dirty, though unlike then, Moon wasn't there to make it better. He felt like it had been years since he showered last. His hair felt like a greasy mess, the red dye on the sides growing out. His hair, in general, seemed to be growing too long for his liking.

He was alone, or close to it. Cheryl helped and was someone to talk to, but she had been there so long the lines of reality had blurred and it was sometimes too much to be around. Acting as if nothing was wrong, as if she was apart of the family; living in a delusion to help her cope.

He missed his room. He missed the apartment above the diner. Now, this time, he was stuck again. His parents weren't the ones behind it, unless he blamed them for the irresponsible nature that compelled them to have him in the first place... which he did, but that was beside the point.

A soft knock on the doorframe behind him made Jared turn around. Cheryl had one of the worst sleep schedules for a human he had ever seen.

"Sabrina and I are going for a walk. She wanted to know if you want to go with us?"

Jared shrugged.

He didn't have much else to do, but he didn't really know how to be around people in general. The constant flow of awkward commentary his brain supplied didn't help with it either.

"Unless you wanted to turn into a popsicle?" Cheryl offered.

He turned back to the window, looking out at the moon one last time before getting up.

He needed to move around before his body mummified itself or something. He didn't even know what would happen given the fact he was unable to feed for so long. It wasn't like he was given a guidebook, and his parents had never taught him anything useful—unless he planned to be a wanted criminal.

"It's not that bad," Jared lied.

He wrapped his arms around himself anyway and followed her out into the hall.

He would be fine.

The house was quiet, and the dark hallways only left the place feeling more eerie than it normally was. Walking in the dark wasn't an issue for him. He could sense where things were. Much like the echolocation bats had, he supposed. When he focused on seeing in the dark it was almost like he could see the vague outline of the overwhelming amount of shit the Graham family acquired over however many fucking years.

"Oh, you got him!" Sabrina clapped her hands.

Jared winced at how loud she was being, not wanting to be found but it also didn't help while using his echolocation, the loud sounds felt like a personal attack on his eardrums. She didn't pay much mind to how quiet the house around them was. She simply grabbed the stuffed animal she normally liked to drag around—Jared was pretty sure it was a bear, but the head was a bunny sewn onto it, so he wasn't all that sure.

"If you could turn into a bat it would be way cooler," Sabrina deadpanned.

Jared had no idea what to do with that information. Turning into a bat didn't seem like it would be all that fun, but then again he wouldn't know. Vampires never did, at least that he was aware of. Even if he could, he could barely think in the human-like form he was currently in let alone turning into something else.

"Sabrina, don't be rude about it," Cheryl muttered before handing her a half-eaten pear.

"I mean flying around like a bat would be pretty cool," Jared shrugged.

"See," Sabrina exclaimed, taking the pear and biting into it. "He agrees."

"Okay," Cheryl sighed and left it at that.

She unlocked the door and one by one they followed her down the steps. The basement was a lot colder than the rest of the house. Something he thought no one could genuinely get used to, yet, the Graham family didn't seem all that bothered. Cheryl had a blanket wrapped over her shoulders, but other than that she didn't seem all that affected either.

Jared learned a lot about the house while being there. He knew about a few of the myths before, but living there was something else. Taking all the stories, reports, and media rumors he had read and thinking nothing more of it than it being a tragic story depending on how much was true. He wasn't expecting to learn just how much of it was real, how some of the lore he thought was just stories passed around at a campfire to scare people turned out to be his current reality.

Wandering around the tunnel of a basement he still didn't want to believe the truth about the house. How sad it was to see a family turn into a living nightmare.

Cheryl helped Sabrina spell her weekly practice words and Jared took notice of how it was one of the only times Sabrina was able to learn—and even then, it wasn't much. Cheryl was the only one teaching her, taking care of her, and she kept her safe from Granny the best she could.

"Why do you bother?" Jared asked, then paused because he didn't mean for it to come out so rude. "I mean, what made you think to start teaching her stuff like that?"

Sabrina ahead of them enough not to overhear him.

Cheryl looked over, through the faint glow of the small candelabra she had lit that did nothing but make her look like a ghost haunting the basement—though the idea wouldn't be a total shock to Jared at this point.

"It helps," Cheryl murmured. "It keeps us both busy, and if we manage to get out and live normal lives again I don't want her to be stuck learning things from the beginning. I can at least teach her some of the basics."

They walked down the hall that never seemed to end and over to the storage rooms. The rooms were filled with junk and left for trash. Most of the things in the basement were better preserved than anywhere else in the house.

Jared didn't understand it. There were boxes labeled and filled with pictures, framed and with a smiling family in them, what he assumed to be the Graham family before moving there. Years before, when they were younger, clean, and from the looks of it once happy at the time of the picture. Something long lost to what became of them since moving back.

He didn't want to turn out like them, to be someone turning into a mindless zombie of Granny's creation; a shell of a person he once was before she got to him.

He didn't want his friends and family to just be a picture he carried around on his or the memories that he had, and the thought left him with the bitter reality of never seeing them again. Of them thinking he ran away or left them at random. But he knew his friends would know better, and he knew Moon would too.

It still didn't help the dizzying feeling of *what if.* The thought being rooted in his brain, the possibility of it alone was enough for him. If he didn't do something to get the hell out of there he would end up just like this family.

Jared pinched the bridge of his nose. "I'm just saying if we can get out of the house one of us could get help—"

"I've tried that," Cheryl cut him off. "I got out and into the woods before being dragged back. They have eyes everywhere all the time."

Cheryl walked closer to him, paranoia in her eyes, as she dropped her voice to a whisper. "I had my phone when I was first here. That night I called the cops, and they told me I was just a teenager pranking them. I tried again the next day before they found my phone. They have a deal with someone high up. They sell to them or something."

"Wait, what the hell does that mean?!" Jared whisper-yelled.

"It means there's someone who comes and deals with the pickups. I assume they're also the ones who keep the house from being noticed."

"So they grow drugs," Jared confirmed.

Cheryl sighed as if he were being particularly difficult. "They grow flowers and herbs."

"I don't—"

Jared was cut off again. "Poppy flowers mostly."

Then it clicked. There were rumors of the farm being once known for the vibrant flowers, but it seemed like they took a different turn at some point when they discovered something that would sell better.

"Oh."

Jared assumed it was something, though he hoped for it to be a little less illegal and more like Granny and wherever she grew in her garden of dead weeds, but he never got a good look at what was behind the backyard. The broken fence left him with a restricted view of most things.

"You don't just get out of a house like this. They'll keep you weak and defenseless, leaving you stuck here even when Granny dies," Cheryl whispered.

It shouldn't have felt so hopeless.

Jared knew he would be stuck there. He had it confirmed on multiple occasions; however, hearing her say it so bluntly—it hit him again. He was really never going to get out of there.

"If you want to know." Cheryl looked over her shoulder. "They have a blonde woman stop by monthly. Avoid her."

Jared nodded even though if he had yet to see her so far, there was a good chance he wouldn't suddenly start now that Cheryl decided to mention it.

"Is she the one who picks up?" Jared whispered.

"Don't know." Cheryl shrugged a bit. "I just know she is meaner than a deer tick stuck up your ass in July."

Jared was *not* going to ask what the fuck that meant... Though the saying did remind him of something Mason would come up with at two in the morning and send it to their group chat or wake them up to inform them of something when they were at sleepovers.

"I think she has something to do with it, but it isn't always just her," Cheryl finally commented.

Jared turned back to the room of junk and looked through a few more boxes as he listened. It was rare to get Cheryl in a talkative mood about the Graham family, and he didn't know if it was her paranoia or if it was the unpleasant knowledge of it all. He did his best not to push it too far, but at the end of the day, he needed answers. The more he knew the better he could understand how to get the fuck out of there. He was not going to be stuck there.

He couldn't.

Jared rooted through box after box trying to find something to change into that wasn't totally repulsive. If he had to wear his shirt for one more day he was pretty sure it would start to stick to him—and he would be stuck in it forever.

Cheryl handed over the box with old clothes in it, most likely doing the same as he was.

Sabrina helped but was much more interested in the frog knick-knacks she found. It kinda made Jared sick with how normal this was for them. How unbothered they seemed to be while looking through boxes of trash in the dead of night in a basement of a murdering, brainwashing, cursed family.

He swallowed the pit in his throat and grabbed the first flannel he found that didn't have bugs crawling all over it.

He *would* get out.

He had to.

Chapter Ten
Someone Definitely Died Here

Husher Carden – 27, November (Monday)

Husher guessed it had taken an hour of walking.

An hour listening to Mason's comments and walking in the cold. His body buzzed with adrenaline, but he wasn't sure if it was that, if it was because of the fact he was actually following a lead from a rumor, or if it was the eerily bright moon.

He would have known if it was a full moon right?
Though, at the moment, the symptoms he was used to sleeping off seemed a bit too close to the anxiety of possibly finding his best friend after so long; energy rushing through his veins making it so he couldn't truthfully tell what it was.

"How many bodies do you think are buried here, specifically by murder?" Mason questioned.

"Probably not as many as you think there would be." Lee shrugged, unbothered by the question after the last hour.

"What kind of answer is that?" Mason snorted.

"What kind of question was that?" Husher deadpanned.

Mason stepped over a dead tree branch before turning and walking backward. "I mean you can't say you haven't thought about it. Someone is probably dead and buried where you're standing right now."

It was cold, dark, and muddy out. Their phones had long ago gone out of service and wandering in the woods was not nearly as easy as he remembered it being when he was a kid. Thinking about how many people died where he was standing had in fact *not* crossed his mind during the entire walk—so far into the woods...at least until now.

"I can't say that it has, looking for Jared—you know, the whole point we're out here right now—that has been on my mind," Husher explained.

"Ugh, get your panties out of your ass. I was just trying to lighten the mood," Mason groaned. "It's so boring listening to your heartbeats."

Lee flicked her in the arm. "You're a banshee, you don't have enhanced hearing."

"You don't know that for sure," Mason said vaguely.

Husher ignored both of them and looked ahead.

"Worrying so much isn't going to help," Mason put her hands up in defense. "I cope by sarcasm and gaslighting myself into acting as normal as possible."

"We know," Lee sighed.

Husher nodded in agreement, looking past them for a second only to close his eyes for a moment and focused ahead again when he opened them, seeing through the darkness around him. His hazel green eyes turned a shade of gold as he looked ahead.

The vibrant oranges of the autumn trees turned the same shade as everything else in his monochromatic vision. Up ahead there was a clearing, it was small but the wooded area seemed dense after that.

Husher blinked and his eyesight was back to normal.

When they made it to the clearing he could see the cluster of tall trees that loomed over them past the defoliated area. It looked too much like the way they had just come, despite following the map just as Lee said. They knew where they were going, Lee took the time to print out the directions with the shortest path—knowing their phone wouldn't work so far into the woods.

"So who wants to hear my impressions?" Mason asked.

Lee and Husher both looked at each other horrified.

"Joking," Mason shook her head. "But wow, you could have just said no."

Though Husher knew just as well as anyone that Mason would have still done her impressions if she got bored enough. It never went well and they all knew it, including her.

By the two-hour mark, Husher had only been stuck in his own head. Mostly, he wondered, *Why would Jared have walked this path to begin with?* The question and various similar ones stuck on repeat with each step.

Sure, it was most likely a lead to nowhere; however, if Jared did come out to the middle of the woods, Husher didn't understand why. If Jared already walked into the woods that night he went missing, he couldn't have gotten *that* lost. Jared could see in the dark. Sure it was more of a sound thing like bats, and every time he explained it, Husher was left more confused than before.

However, it still meant Jared wasn't out in the dark.

He *could* have gotten lost due to his poor directional skills, but nothing made any sense, no matter how much he thought about it.

Husher stopped, not realizing he was in the lead somehow, and his friends bumped into him.

"What the fuck, dude?" Mason demanded, almost tripping behind him.

There was something about the eerie feeling of them not being alone that always made this ten times as scary. The hair on his arms standing up as he tried to figure out if he should be concerned about the sound or if it was just the woods creepy atmosphere getting to him. His instincts warned him how bad of an idea this all was.

It was faint and the weather had most likely covered the majority of it up, but there was something in the air. He looked over to Lee to see if they smelt it too or if Husher's mind was seriously starting to make things up.

Lee had turned off the slight path—or rather the muddy trail with slightly less plant growth—and was looking down at the ground.

Husher tilted his head in confusion before walking over to them. When he looked down where Lee was he froze. Footprints. But it was just some hiker, since the boot print was nothing like the print of any of their shoes and didn't look like it'd come from Jared's hightops.

It was pointless.

Lots of people hiked around the area, maybe not this far off the path but living so close to the Appalachian trail he shrugged it off.

He knew better than to get his hopes up, and he was now pretty sure it was a full moon which only enhanced what he was feeling.

He needed to get out of there.

There was no way Jared went all the way out in the mud just to find a house he had heard rumors about. He could have waited and dragged all of them out there and he would have worn shoes he didn't care about; not the red hightops he had customized, not the ones he added mini pins too for fun.

"I think we should just go back."

"Bitch," Mason coughed.

"What?" Husher turned to her confused, but not surprised.

"Oh, I meant to say *little* bitch or do you prefer—"

"Stop it, both of you." Lee stood up and sighed. "We aren't stopping until we get there."

"Why? He wouldn't have walked out here," Husher questioned. "He was just going for a *short* walk, we all know he wouldn't walk for hours—especially not on a whim."

Mason shrugged. "Two hours later maybe he got lost, dude. You know he is shit with directions."

"Not helping," Husher muttered.

Mason shrugged and crossed her arms. "Never said I was going to be helpful."

"Let's just keep going, and if it's nothing then I will buy you breakfast," Lee added. It was almost like they were treating Husher as one of their cousins who both refused to listen to anyone without a bribe.

Lee turned back knowing just as well as Husher did that he would listen to them. Not even a few seconds after that Lee turned back to the route did they trip and fall to the side of the path. Mud covered Lee as they fell down the slight incline they were on. The slippery leaves didn't help make the path any easier to walk on, especially in the dark. Husher quickly walked over to help Lee up, minding where he stepped so he didn't end up in the mud too.

Mason followed after, but her laughter made the offer of help seem a little less sincere.

Lee was on the ground, their glasses on the edge of their nose before they pushed them up with the back of their wrist. Lee's hands were covered in mud as they pushed down into the ground to balance themself enough to get up—but they paused midway.

Husher and Mason offered out their hands to help, but Lee shook their head. They sat back as they pulled up a muddy phone. Husher cringed; it would take forever to get their phone cleaned and even then it probably wouldn't work—but it wasn't Lee's phone.

"Well fucko, look what we found." Mason punched Husher in the arm.

He winced for a moment at the pain before looking at the phone. He honestly didn't want to get his hopes up again only to have them shattered. Lots of people could have walked this path; maybe it was from one of the dead people Mason was going on about.

Husher shook his head, knowing they were all thinking it. "You can't be sure it's his."

Mason punched him again and wow, he was definitely going to have bruises by the end of this walk.

"Who else do you know who has a bright-ass red phone case with a skeleton sticker on it?!" Mason questioned.

"Come on, it has to mean we're close!" Lee exclaimed.

Husher took the phone while Mason helped Lee get up. He tried to turn the phone on, but given it had been out there for eighty-four days, the battery was long dead.

Husher ignored the sick feeling he had and put the device into his backpack. He followed Lee the rest of the way through the wooded area as it became denser before coming to another clearing. This time tall grass and weeds came up to his knees, and the plants with thorns clung to his pants with nearly each step.

This time it was Husher who walked into Mason and Lee, nearly taking them all to the ground with him as he tried to regain his balance.

"Dude," Mason grumbled.

"Shush!" Lee informed them both.

Before Husher could question it he looked ahead to where Lee was. It was still dark out, a few more hours until the sun rose if he had to guess; however, even without his wolf he could see the house up ahead.

"Be quiet," Lee reminded them.

Mason rolled her eyes but didn't say anything.

Husher followed as they walked closer, using the tall grass and trees around them to hide. Husher couldn't smell anything, but the rainy weather and full moon didn't help him with that either.

The house ahead was definitely long abandoned. Two of the front windows were nothing more than crackled glass, holes in them and left forgotten like the rest of the house. Once white siding turned different shades of green and brown as it got worse piece by piece, falling off at parts and rotting at others. Plants long ago growing up the front porch, thick vines and bushes surrounded the house, trailing their way up as they consumed most of the place.

Husher had no idea what they were planning; he hadn't thought they would get this far if he was being honest.

Should they go in?

He knew they had a mix of daggers and maybe a sword with them if Lee somehow shoved it into their backpack—though Husher doubted that would help. Perhaps, it was better than nothing. Mason was the only one who could fight, if they ran into someone while in the house he and Lee wouldn't do so well. While Husher could look intimidating, he knew if it came down to a fist fight he would most certainly lose.

They watched the house for a moment. It didn't seem like there was anyone living there, looking as if it had been left forgotten for years. Assuming it looked as bad on the inside as it did on the outside there was no way someone could live there without falling through floorboards or being eaten by the plants around it that were trying to take over.

"What's that thing over there?" Mason whispered.

Lee must have looked over just as Husher did because once they saw what Mason was pointing to they both jumped back.

There was someone walking out of the house. Husher focused on them the best he could without using his wolf eyes. The last thing he needed was someone seeing glowing gold eyes in the woods. The person looked to be Mason's height, they were white—so white, Husher thought he was in some dramatic vampire movie and the person who walked out had the skin of a killer—it was nearly sparkling. He had dark hair Husher assumed to be some shade of brown, his shoulders were hunched, his gaze kept to the ground, kicking at the dying grass as he made his way over to a rotting fence. Surprisingly, he unlatched the fence gate and walked through, scanning the area behind him before turning back and closing the gate after him.

"If we're wrong, we're dead," Lee whispered.

"If we're right, we might also be dead," Husher corrected.

Mason flipped them both off and walked closer to the house all the while staying hidden in the woods as much as she could. Husher looked over to Lee who seemed to have the same worried look as him.

"We could just leave her here?" Husher joked.

"She would find her way back," Lee commented, sarcastically.

As much as he wanted to lighten the mood the thought of going closer to the house was sickening.

With a sigh they followed Mason, walking around the property while keeping their distance. When they walked closer to the house Husher noticed a screen door on the side. The door appeared to be open and for a minute it didn't sink in how bad an idea this all was. Husher looked to Mason and Lee who both seemed to notice the door too. He didn't know how much time they had before the person from earlier returned. It would be too risky to go in... but they didn't come all this way for nothing.

Lee was the one to push it open, looking in the dark house only for a moment before stepping foot inside. Mason held the door open as she stepped inside the house after them. Husher was last to go in, thinking they were *all* going to die as his shoe made contact with the floor.

Chapter Eleven
Everything Was Rather Concerning

Jared Baylor – 27, November (Monday)

J ared had lost track of how long they had spent in the basement looking through the Graham family things only to find a slightly less smelly flannel and a concerning amount of bugs.

It wasn't worth it.

However, it did kill a little time he could have spent thinking about the past and freezing by the window. The things he found as positives about his day were truly getting concerning, more than they usually were.

"It's better than nothing," Cheryl shrugged.

"The fact a spider was on that and we are counting two shirts and a blanket as a win is an all-new kind of depressing."

"One of the reasons I don't come down here often. There really isn't much, kinda just assumed they brought it here from when Brandy and Terry moved in with Granny, but the more I look it seems like there are things even older down here," Cheryl explained.

She still seemed too unbothered about it all for Jared's liking. Jared half thought maybe she had to stay calm about things. It would be easy to turn into one of Granny's favorites if she didn't guard her mind.

Cheryl turned to get Sabrina, but she was sleeping on not one, but two of her frog knick-knacks that she had been playing with earlier.

"I can take the stuff if you want to take her?" Jared offered.

Cheryl nodded. "Yeah, that works for me."

It was still dark out when he snuck back up, the house looking just as creepy as it did before. The broken windows let in odd streams of light, most of the windows being blocked off, a few boarded over and letting in less light than

Jared would have liked. Slowly, he opened the basement door and held it open while Cheryl carried Sabrina up and to her playroom. Closing doors in a house so silent, Jared almost thought taking two pans from the kitchen and smashing them together would have been equally as loud no matter how hard he tried to be quiet.

Jared walked to Sabrina's playroom, ignoring the creek of the floor with each step. Cheryl let Sabrina take most of the couch while she took up the other side. Jared quietly left the other shirt and the blanket they found with them and kept the flannel for himself.

The house was just as quiet when Jared turned back to go upstairs. He was careful with each step, avoiding the extra loud stairs or floorboards learning the hard way which made the most noise. He knew the last thing he needed to do was wake anyone up as he made his way back to the extra room.

He knew by now Jordan would be leaving just a little before sunrise to check the garden behind the house. The same garden that apparently he was correct to assume was drug-related and not just him joking because he had watched too many fictional shows for the situation to feel real.

Jared had no idea what they would be doing with what were most likely dead plants, but he did his best not to overthink it. The Graham family didn't make any sense to him. The fact they grew and sold drugs was not even close to being their more concerning traits. If he kept thinking about them he was only going to go back to the kitchen and grab one of the frying pans and hit himself in the head with it just to have a second of peace.

Maybe the moon was affecting him too. Full moons didn't just mess with werewolves. Even humans acted a little strange on nights with full moons, as if the energy was too much for any of them. Or maybe he was just tired and going down too much of a rabbit hole to make sense of himself.

Jared settled in between the wall and a pile of junk where he could see out the window a little as he lay back. It was just about as comfortable as his space in the garage, but at least he was able to look outside and not at a ceiling—he was pretty sure it was going to collapse on him any second.

He thought for a moment he could finally get to sleep, but it seemed his brain had other ideas. As if the constant thoughts about nothing had ever made sense to him before. As if he could think about anything but what his mind wanted him to.

This time all he could replay was the night that he was taken. He was so sure the night would end differently. So sure he would end it by inhaling a gallon of cotton candy ice cream, quite possibly regretting his existence yet again.

It was the little things. Fear was nothing new, but things built up, filling Jared's lungs with sludge as the world began to feel all too suffocating.

There wasn't one particular thing that set him off, but rather a cluster of little reasons that crashed their way into his skull, the urge to just blurt it out—to admit his secret—to breathe it out into the world.

The September air was enough to have shivers creep down his spine, the urge to hyperventilate but not daring to breathe too loud—not daring to admit to anything. His palms sweaty and cold, his fingers were numb and if not for the black nail polish that covered them he would have been able to see his nails turn a muted blue. His nerves engulfed him completely.

Jared went with Husher for a walk around the town, something they normally did if the weather was good enough. They always went for walks in the end anyway though, the winter being the only season they didn't have a routine since the weather was a little too unpredictable. And much like all the other nights, Jared couldn't help but let his mind wander away from him. It happened a lot when it was just the two of them and the question or statement was always on the tip of Jared's tongue.

Then he would be reminded who he was, the side eyed looks he used to get, the hushed whispers about his parents selling again—things didn't work out well for him.

Jared was reluctant to head back home once they walked around the block twice, as they normally did. The urge to just get lost in conversation, babbling on about their day no matter how unexciting—to fill the void of worry that wormed its way into his head.

This night only made it clear that they had been friends for years. Silence with Husher didn't make him feel uncomfortable like it always did when he was left to fend for himself in conversations. He had been friends with Husher since they were kids. However, unlike his friendships with Lee and Mason—who he was friends with for nearly as long—Jared never felt like the world was put on pause when he was with them, but it did when he was with the blond. It didn't feel like he lost track of time with them. That the earth stopped spinning for a moment and he was able to breathe even if he was pretty sure if the world did such a thing he would unarguably not be breathing.

Husher Carden was the exception for too many things in Jared's life.

Lee and Mason were just as much of his friends as Husher was; however, Jared wasn't worried about staring too long... noticing the flecks of gold in his hazel green eyes, and he wasn't worried about sleeping too close when he spent the night at their house—even if they had done that since grade school and sharing a bed was normal for them. For fuck's sake he even stupidly used his named as his password, followed by his birthday—march ninth.

Jared knew better to think anything would become of it.

The first time it happened he thought he was seeing things. He thought he was turning into his mom and his mind was truly hating him for making him believe such a sick joke.

"You're just being a nerd about it again. With your vamp-brain and stuff," Husher stated as if that made total sense to him.

"All I said was he would be a leo—which makes sense since he is basically the star of the damn show," Jared stated again.

Husher threw a piece of popcorn at him. "Nerd."

"How the fuck does that even make—you know what, never mind."

Jared sighed and threw the piece of popcorn back at him.

Only ending it with a popcorn battle, of course.

It was one of the many instances time itself seemed to freeze. Forgetting the outside anxiety and being able to relax until the perpetual doom loomed over him again.

While he knew Husher was gay it never affected him. Just like he knew Mason had two dads and Lee lived with their grandma and aunt.

Looking back, he should have noticed it the one—day in school when they were told to draw their future selves and Husher, the fucking idiot, drew *him* by his side. Jared never noticed if the feelings were returned. All he knew was falling—no—tripping and then crash landing for his best friend was *not* something he needed.

If he lost Husher, he lost everything.

Jared shoved his free hand into his hoodie, he thumbed over a piece of rose quartz as if it would save him. The light pink crystal doing little to help be anything but a fidget toy as Jared walked along. All that he could think of was how stupid he was for assuming he could even say something about it, going so far as to ask Moon about it since she was one of the few people who knew about his secret or rather one of the few people Jared confirmed his secret to.

Instead of her saying something helpful like, "*Don't mess up a perfectly good friendship,*" or anything along those lines, he was handed a light pink crystal and sent on his way.

Jared kept a hold onto the rose quartz questioning why he always felt so damn awkward.

He didn't even know at first that he had a crush on his best friend until Husher got his first boyfriend in middle school and Jared was not the best version of himself during those two weeks. While they broke up soon enough, Jared still hated himself for how happy he was when he got the news it was over.

"You're going to have to tell him," Moon informed him after a particularly long movie night where he was in full-on crisis mode.

Jared fell down face-first onto the couch. "I really don't. I can suffer and die."

Even without seeing her face, Jared knew Moon rolled her eyes at his comment as if he was being particularly difficult. He seriously didn't need to discover such things about himself when liking people was never something that interested him before.

He didn't like anyone, at least not like that.

While he could notice someone who looked nice that was about it; he never felt like he needed to make it anything more. The thought of having to do so much as hug another person made him want to shrink in on himself.

Moon sat down on the edge of the couch, pushing his feet off the cushion to make room.

"It's easy, just tell him you're an idiot."

"Wow, thanks for the love and support," Jared muttered.

His plans didn't seem to work out, considering he was pretty sure Husher was the only one who *didn't* know or suspect something at that point.

Jared knew that Lee had figured it out in high school and Mason soon after that and how she would only smirk when she got them to sit beside each other. Which helped with nothing other than him getting knowing looks sent his way whenever Husher wasn't paying attention.

The night Jared was taken was the night he had planned to tell him the truth.

He just couldn't get the words out. When they got news of getting into the same college—the plans of them getting an apartment with him and Mason closer to school was something that looked to be some kind of reality.

But then his mind thought it was a good time to remind him—as if he could forget—that if he told Husher his secret and it went well then he would be over whatever the weird feeling of skeletons punching him in the heart was. The same skeletons that haunted him since he graduated high school and the feelings that were still fucking there, stubborn and annoying as ever. He genuinely couldn't take it anymore.

Jared opened his eyes and looked up to the sky, even if he knew it could very well end with him falling face-first onto the pavement. It would have been better than thinking about all the reasons there was no point in trying, better than just staying there in a sour mood.

He felt as hopeful as he was depressed.

He needed to go the fuck back to the diner before it was too late. He was no closer to figuring out how the hell to manage that. So he let Husher walk away and made an excuse to keep walking even when he just wanted to go home and bury himself into his bed and never leave.

Reality wasn't much better than his memories, and being stuck in a house that smelled like shit while he was drugged with herbs that made him feel like he was covered in poison ivy from the inside out seemed just as frustrating as the hunger pains that ached behind his fangs.

He was stuck with nothing to do next, and while he never liked fairy tales nor did he see himself as a princess in need of saving, it would be nice.

He didn't want to save himself again.

He already had.

It wasn't fair he had to keep doing it.

He picked at the box to his left and tried not to think about how much he failed his first week of being there. He could have gotten out if he didn't fuck up his step. Now his thoughts felt like mush. Everything hurt and he felt much too tired to care anymore.

Chapter Twelve
Don't Breathe

Husher Garden – 27, November (Monday)

Husher thought that being the last one to walk in the house was somehow worse than being the first.

He thought for sure that the person who he had seen earlier would come back and he would be the one left to fight them off.

Like the times he would go to a haunted maze and somehow every time Husher would find himself the last one in their group—which would have been fine, until they turned around and he had managed to be the lead at *every* wrong turn.

"Ew!" Mason cringed.

Lee quickly shushed her, though Husher had to agree with Mason. The house was past the years of being trashed and left to rot to a level of decay that Husher had never seen before in a house. The beauty it might have once had was gone.

It was hard to think the place was once loved and taken care of, as the inside of the house matched the outside with its rotting charm.

Breathing felt atrocious, and every breath smelled worse. The lingering, thick smell of something rotting was enough to make Husher's eyes water, like Jared's during allergy season.

"It smells as if rotting flesh had sex with a very sweaty locker room and the house is the result," Mason groaned.

Husher wasn't sure how or why that made sense, however, he couldn't help but think the smell alone made *him* want to leave. He was no stranger to bad smells in his line of work. Going out of town for a free house cleaning every few weeks to help someone who needed it, he was bound to find some not-so-pleasant smells. Most of the houses had rooms piled with trash that had been there for years, yet he didn't think he would ever get used to the smells of this house. It felt like they clung to his soul at this point.

The small hallway they were in was lined with muddy footprints so bad he thought they were still outside and walking on the muddy paths littered with dead plants and leaves. It was like the floor was dried with layers of mud and replaced with even muddier footprints.

Husher stayed as quiet as he could as they walked farther into the house.

He made sure the screen door behind him closed slowly and quietly—or at least the best he could manage with its squeaky hinges. The floor creaked below them, and for a moment Husher wondered if it was safe to be in there.

Then he remembered they were trespassing and the person who had left the house could very well come back any second—making the whole thing a disaster waiting to happen.

Nothing about it was safe and he damn well knew it.

He pulled his shirt up a little, enough to cover his nose and mute the smell ever so slightly. It wasn't much, but it helped a little with the scent of rotting flesh.

Fighting the urge to throw up that was worse than the time Husher took one of the trick candies Ava got for her birthday. He didn't know at the time that the identical looking candies were in fact flavored in a revolting way, and instead of being met with the coconut flavor he *thought* he was getting he got the one that tasted like spoiled milk.

Now, though, Husher would have killed for the spoiled milk candy over the putrid stench coming from the house he stepped into.

Husher looked around only to come to a halting stop at the same time Lee pushed him back. At the end of the hall, there was a kitchen where an older woman was chopping up something into pieces on the counter.

When Husher crept forward he couldn't tell what the creature once was, most likely some kind of farm animal, but he couldn't smell anything but filth since the moment he stepped into the house.

He felt like he was going to be sick.

He looked to his friends silently asking what to do only to catch a grin on Mason's face. Husher looked back to Lee who he was pretty sure was wearing a matching horrified expression on their face. The moment Mason reached for her daggers Husher lunged forward and grabbed her, wrapping his arms around her shoulders while Lee hesitantly grabbed the hilt of the daggers. They shook their head in warning. Mason tensed for a moment but let go of her weapons, elbowing Husher lightly to let go seconds later.

Slowly, they backed down the short hallway they came from and in a state of pure panic ducked into the door on their right. Husher didn't notice it before, but given it was either that or go out the loud screen door they all picked the unknown door.

Husher let go of Mason and Lee handed back her daggers once the door was shut. The smell was a little better, leaving Husher feeling slightly less nauseous. The small room was dark and just as dirty as what Husher had assumed the rest of the house would be like. There were cobwebs within cobwebs, creating small suburbs for the arachnids. He knew if one touched him he would lose it and give their hiding spot away immediately.

He shivered at the thought.

The moment of silence probably was only several seconds long but to Husher it felt like hours as the blond haltingly noticed there were eyes looking back at him. Lee and Mason seemed to freeze by his side as they both locked eyes with a kid maybe eleven or twelve years old. She had long matted brown hair and looked sickly pale. Husher thought maybe she was an undead, close to a vampire but unable to walk in the sun—and more related to myths about zombies—if such creatures existed.

Husher listened closely and her heartbeat seemed human. Werewolves had slightly slower heartbeats, elves had quicker heartbeats, banshees and witches were the closest to humans and undetectable as a supernatural person, and vampires had low and steady heartbeats.

The spawn looked them up and down. Husher didn't know if running out of the door at this point would be a good idea or if the window would be a more effective way of getting the hell out of there.

Mason looked over to Husher and then back at the kid as if not wanting to lose sight of it. Husher had no idea what they should do, but apparently, Lee was the first to process the situation and the quickest to say something.

"Uh, hi." Lee waved awkwardly.

Mason slapped their arm, nearly slapping Husher who was standing between them. Husher looked around the room. There was something wrong—there were a lot of things wrong, and it felt like this wasn't even the tip of the iceberg. He tried not to freak out. It would do none of them any good and only get them caught by people Husher was pretty sure he didn't want to ever meet.

He could barely process his current situation. Being trapped in an unknown place looking for his best friend who had been missing and their best guess was a house that should have been abandoned years ago—to say something was off was just touching the surface of the problem.

However, there was something his wolf was picking up that he wasn't. It felt familiar, comforting almost; in the same way it felt to walk in the rain on a summer day. It was strange given where he was standing.

It took him a minute to ground himself.

When he looked around the room he did his best to take a breath, taking in his senses without overstimulating himself with an overload of anxiety and irritation. It felt like everything was just a bit too heightened and a bad time to realize while the worst of it was over, the lingering buzz across his skin and shake of his hands was most likely due to the full moon he had forgotten about. He added it to the list of things he could freak out about later. Along with the cobwebs around him that were just a little too close for his comfort.

The weight of feeling like something was off wasn't enough to clue him in on what exactly it was. He looked around the decaying room. The trash and rotting foundation of a house had little to offer him that was useful.

He looked over to his friends, but both seemed to be focused on figuring out what to do with the kid. Most likely thinking about how they could find out if Jared was there and how they could leave without anyone seeing or hearing them there.

Husher was about to ignore the feeling his wolf was insisting on when he finally figured it out.

When he saw it, he was surprised he hadn't noticed it sooner.

The kid was holding a stuffed animal that Husher was too scared to ask what the hell it even was—but on its matted fur was a pin. A small pin, painted with detail. A black triangle at the left side, white at the top, a royal purple in line perfectly in the middle, and a light gray at the bottom.

Husher would have recognized the pin anywhere. He was there when Jared had tried—and failed—to paint it at least six different times until Miss Moon grabbed it from him and did it herself. He always wore it on his shoes along with the two other pins he made. Most with plants or mushrooms since Mason liked to customize gifts to them all, pins the go-to gifts for any special occasions and/or birthdays.

Mason seemed to follow his line of vision and quickly grabbed his arm before he even noticed himself sinking to the floor. Lee quickly did the same, only to look back at Husher with a blank face.

They pulled him up and did their best to keep him steady, but Husher didn't notice anything but the damn pin.

His heart sank.

His whole world tilted a bit as he processed the implications. Jared had actually been there… and all Husher was able to do was spiral down questionable thoughts as to what happened to his best friend.

Jared was there.

"I would *not* sit on the floor, dude." Mason tugged him up. Lee stayed quiet but did the same until Husher was steady enough to stand on his own.

He shook his head in disbelief. He knew that if he thought about it then he would have to think about how they ignored the muddy path. How no one could track Jared's scent. How no location spell worked. It was like the house was a dead end, the edge of town and a history of a long-forgotten family.

He had been so close and they weren't able to do anything.

What if it was too late and the reason they couldn't track him was because there wasn't anything left of him to track?

No, Husher was *not* going to think that way. They did not come all this way just to give up and leave it to the depressive train of thoughts. He shook his head as if that could get him out of the fog that was taking over his brain.

"We need to get out of here," Husher muttered.

"No shit." Mason slapped him.

Which seemed to help ever so slightly ground him from his thoughts. Just because it was something, a hint, a clue that they were headed in the correct direction. The information confirmed to Husher they wouldn't be leaving any time soon. He needed to get farther into the house and see if there was any trace left of Jared. He was not going to leave until he got the answers he needed.

It was then that the kid decided to grin at them.

It was right out of his nightmares as the spawn pointed to them like something he could only see in his nightmares. Husher, Mason, and Lee were surely going to be the ones killed in some gruesome way that Husher always had to look away from in any gory horror movie.

"Kid, where'd you get the pin?" Mason asked, pointing to the stuffed animal.

The kid didn't answer and for a moment Husher wondered if she spoke English, but the kid tucked the stuffed animal under her arm and brought her hands up to her face, pointer fingers down and in front of her grinning face, as if she had fangs.

Husher held his breath, trying very hard not to freak out about the new information.

Lee nodded. "Okay, uh, I think we should see if he's still here and leave."

Mason rolled her eyes and in a forced sarcastic tone she asked, "Do you?"

Husher felt the rooted worry take over.

Chapter Thirteen
Roadkill for Dinner Again...
How Lovely

When Jared woke up, he heard a knife being vio-lently thrown into the counter as if Granny was feeling particularly stabby that day.

The thunderous noise of Granny cooking or preparing dinner was something Jared never wanted to hear again. It made his entire body go cold—well, colder than his aching limbs already were.

All he could do was feel bad for whatever poor road kill she caught, and while it was already dead, she felt the need to chop and mutilate it into mush. It was enough for him to want to switch to vegetarianism whenever he ate human food.

The room he was in was barely lit with morning light, leaving lingering shadows around all the junk in the room. He closed his eyes again, knowing he wouldn't go back to sleep with the loud knife skills happening in the kitchen, but he wasn't ready to leave his safe spot in the house.

He breathed in the cool morning breeze from the open window; however, it did nothing to help his freezing limbs. The chills it sent through his bones were welcomed at this point. It was enough to keep him from drowning in his own head. It felt like one of the few moments of peace he would have for the day. Just a few minutes that he didn't have to be afraid of whatever bullshit Granny had planned to do with his life.

He would dread knowing he would be forced to eat whatever she made later. He would ignore the same food that was laced with herbs that made his body feel like it was turning inside out and rolled in hot ash.

There wasn't much he could do about it at this point. Maybe he could convince Cheryl she could leave and they could take down the Graham family, but if it hadn't worked so far, he wasn't sure what made today any differ-ent.

Jared buried himself deeper into the makeshift bed he had, using the flannel he found the night before as a blanket and his arms behind his head as a pillow. It was by far the most comfortable he was able to get, but that wasn't saying much.

The sun offered little warmth and he made note not to stay in it too long and make himself sick.

Jared knew he would go back out to the garage for the rest of the day, hiding away with smelly blankets that did nothing for him when he had no body heat to regulate, to begin with. In the meantime, he needed just a moment longer in the sunlight. Feeling the tingles across his skin and the colors that made their way into the brightening sky.

Then, as the sun turned from orange to a hurtful, eye-burning yellow, the moment of peace was shattered as Cheryl burst into the room. Brandy was only down the hall locked in her room. Terry was either outside with Jordan or in the basement helping prepare for the family dinner.

"What are you—" Jared was quickly cut off.

The all too familiar rush of panic rushed through his veins.

Cheryl wouldn't go out of her routine; it was how she kept herself safe and sane. Jared braced himself for the bad news she would most likely deliver—even if a small part of him hoped she would say she figured a weak point in the house and they were leaving.

He knew better than to hope.

It was a damning thought for him to have.

Cheryl shushed him. "We have a problem."

Jared blinked.

They had quite a few problems, none of it being news to him. He was quite literally hiding from a family who abhorred the *monsters* all the while who refused to let him leave and believed he should have never been born. At least they could agree on *one* thing.

"Bad way to word it," she shook her head, catching what she said.

Quickly she rushed into the room, making sure to shut the door behind her as quietly and quickly as she could. Jared didn't think he wanted to know what was so problematic that caused her to be walking closer and over the piles of forgotten things, abandoning her usual morning routine.

"Terry was in a bad mood this morning. I heard him leave before Jordan went to the field," Cheryl explained.

Jared hoped they fucking stayed out there all day, maybe even had a painful and deadly accident while they were out there. It wasn't the nicest of thoughts, but he didn't take them back. He really was hoping for some quicker karma on those bitches. Or maybe he should have hoped for the magic ability to burst them in flames while they were out there if he could. He would have to ask Miss Moon if she had such a spell—if he ever saw her again.

"Brandy is in the attic. She came down last night and watched Sabrina sleep and it triggered her again," Cheryl whispered.

Jared didn't see what the problem was.

The woman led her family into a house that took and ripped at the edges of all and any happiness. It was like being in the damned pits of Tartarus; listening to such toxic behavior and proceeding to do nothing about it would mess anyone up.

"Cheryl, she did that two days ago," Jared said blankly. "She'll keep doing it because that's just how her body deals with unresolved trauma I guess."

He wasn't honestly sure why Brandy did what she did. It should have been easy for her to leave—she wasn't affected by the house meanwhile Jared felt like what was left of his soul was being drained into nothingness. She wasn't physically stuck, she was mentally stuck. Whatever Granny had drilled into her skull like some fucked up lobotomy had clearly gotten the woman messed up.

If what Cheryl had told him over his hellish time there, it was what started as—or what should have been—a check-in of Brandy's mother-in-law turned into a life-time stay in Hell for her and her family. Seeing how gone Brandy was, it probably didn't take much for Granny to train her to do what she said.

Cheryl shook her head and looked a bit constipated as she opened her mouth to say something then quickly closed it only to try again.

"There's someone in the house," Cheryl managed to say.

Jared sat up so quickly that the room spun around him. The compilations of it all coming back to him from when he first walked into the hallway near the kitchen.

If there was someone there, they could help them get out—or it could be someone like him who would be bound to the house until the hag chopping roadkill in the kitchen was dead—and even then Jared didn't know if it would get him out.

"Are you sure?" Jared asked once the room was done spinning. He did not want to add throwing up to the list of things he didn't want to do today.

Cheryl nodded.

He was used to listening to the creaks of the house; paying attention to footsteps and who they belonged to was sometimes what kept him safe. There was no way someone was in the house without him hearing the loud-ass doors. Downstairs he could only hear the sounds of Granny chopping away at the sad dinner and walking around the kitchen.

It was pointless to try and hear anything with that old hag down there. He would have to get up and try to find them before she did. Maybe he could get out this time. He just didn't know what kind of situation he was walking in on the main floor of the house.

"I'm going to get Sabrina, but we need to get them out before Granny finds out," Cheryl informed him.

"How do you know it isn't just the drop-off guy or whoever?" Jared asked. There was no way he wanted to meet him or the blonde Cheryl had talked about before. Jared had the Graham family to deal with. He did not need to add more names to the list of people he hoped had their socks filled with fire ants.

She shook her head and looked even more constipated at that point.

Jared sighed and got up.

Feeling the cold numbness of his joints as he moved, the sun had done next to nothing to help warm him up enough to move quickly.

"Okay," Jared murmured. "I'll distract Granny. You get Sabrina, and if we run into the dumbass who walked into this shithole, we will scare them out... easy."

It was too early, and he was too tired and hungry for this to be his life.

He looked around the room and found an old shovel he had stashed there one night when Granny was being particularly adamant about him coming down for family dinner.

"That would work." Cheryl nodded.

Quietly, they made their way out of the room and into the dark hall. Walking down the steps was always a nightmare, especially when each step felt like he was wearing the goth boots Mason got him for his birthday one year. He always had to think about it when he took his next step. Having to remember which steps were loud and which were louder was nothing but stressful. Cheryl never seemed to have a problem with it, making sure to step more on her toes than with the heel of her foot to help soften the sound. She was nearly silent as she walked.

Jared, on the other hand, was sweating by the time he made it to the last step without it creaking loud enough to alert Granny.

Cheryl looked back for a moment and Jared nodded for her to continue forward. He wasn't sure what they were going to do, but if all else failed, he had the shovel. He would just have to make sure if he had to use it for Granny or any of the Graham family he hit them hard enough that they stayed down long enough for him to hide again.

Slowly, Jared followed Cheryl, stepping in her footprints as she headed towards the extra room on the main floor. Holding his breath as he walked past Granny, her back turned as she wielded a dull knife. He cringed at the snapping sound of bone.

He didn't dare breathe even as he stepped out of sight and into the hallway.

Cheryl opened the door quickly and quietly before halting to a stop and nearly sending the shovel to the ground when Jared ran into her. He kept his grasp and tried not to make a sound as he slowly breathed, his body freezing out of panic.

Sabrina was awake and staring at them with a grin that only confirmed Jared's fear of children.

It was an unsettling creature, for a human.

He needed to stay focused; they needed to get Sabrina and then find whoever was in the house before Terry or Granny noticed them.

Cheryl dragged him into the room before he could take notice of the other people in there with them. He was manhandled—womanhandled—into the room as Cheryl closed the door behind them.

"What the fu—" He shut up when he looked up.

The nightmare was familiar to him by now. Seeing his friends find him only to be killed by Granny and made into her stew seconds later. Seeing them always looked so real, to the point he thought he could smell the pine of Husher, the hint of sage Lee had, even the scent of gas/motor oil Mason always had even on days she wasn't working. It was the kind of nightmare that always left him wishing he never went to sleep in the first place. It was like he was playing a cruel joke on himself when he saw their faces. When he let himself believe it was real and that he was finally safe only to turn around and be traumatized by whatever detailed picture his brain wanted to paint for him.

He backed up.

He could feel the tears filling his eyes as he tried to blink them away.

Instead, he ended up backing up into the door and dropping the shovel. Cheryl quickly caught it, or at least he thought she caught it. He never heard it fall, only the ringing in his ears that felt more like a loud kazoo playing on top of his ear drum.

Jared hated his mind.

He hated how cruel his nightmares were, how real they always were and how quickly they turned out to be like his life. He just wanted to go home—he *needed* to go home. He wanted to leave this place if he didn't die before then.

"You have to be quiet," Cheryl whispered.

Jared felt a silent sob leave his body. He had no control of himself at the moment. If this was a nightmare he just needed to wake up.

Chapter Fourteen
Granny's Sweet Hospitality

Husher Garden – 27, November (Monday)

Husher was more panicked than the second time he accidentally threw a pie into the mayor's wife's face.

The rush of panic made him hold his breath as they heard the footsteps approaching the door.

There were two people at least walking toward them and Husher knew that logically it made no sense hiding behind Mason given the height difference, but it didn't help the fear of who might be on the other side of the door. When the doorknob turned, Husher felt fine. It was as if in a blink of an eye his wolf was calming him. His senses picked up on something his mind was too stubborn or ignorant to fully acknowledge. His wolf, on the other hand, looked at things a little differently. It was like a gut feeling that liked to sometimes slap him in the face with unforgiving news. It made for a great vibe check for anyone he met if needed. Or sometimes it calmed him down, taking the abundance of anxiety and forcing him to listen instead of letting the unwanted thoughts drown him in his own head. In that moment Husher listened to his inner beta that seemed to notice before he did as the door opened it was okay.

An unknown woman with a long braid walked in, and just as he thought his wolf was still acting up because of the full moon, a slightly shorter figure walked in behind her and Husher genuinely thought he was imagining things.

Jared was alive.

Jared was right there.

Jared was... panicking.

He was dirty, much like the woman and the kid who was smiling creepier than a porcelain doll in a haunted house at night. Jared had on an oversized flannel and the t-shirt he was wearing was ripped at the bottom, the dark fabric wrapped around his thigh. His black jeans were marked with dirt and his hoodie was nowhere in sight.

His hair was longer, the red on the sides grown out enough to see his dark brown roots. Husher felt like he was shot with adrenaline when he saw him, like the time Mason had stabbed him in the thigh with an Epi-Pen because he accidentally ate real crab and not imitation.

He couldn't breathe.

But when he saw that Jared was panicking he ignored his own sudden panic, fighting the urge to rush forward and to wrap him in a hug that he would never let go from.

Husher knew it was him.

He fucking knew he was alive, he knew that he—shit, he was sobbing. Husher walked forward slowly. He felt shaky as if any minute Jared would disappear in front of him.

It was really him.

He found him.

While Husher still felt like his breathing was all over the place he did his best to ignore the feeling, the toxic air long forgotten as he stepped forward slowly to not corner or scare the vampire, he needed to make sure Jared was okay.

"No, no, no, it isn't real," Jared sobbed. "It's just a nightmare."

Husher swallowed down his own broken sob; he needed to get through to him and he needed to get him out of there. Jared needed to know he was not imagining things. He stepped in front of Jared making sure not to touch him. Husher remembered the panic attacks he had and most of the time Jared didn't like to be touched without approving of it first.

"Hey," Husher whispered.

Jared shakily turned into himself, trying to get as small as he could. He shook his head in disbelief, panic laced in his voice as he spoke.

"You're not real."

Husher tuned out the others in the room.

If someone was going to harm them, they would have done it by now. It was like no one else in the room was there. Husher could have walked right into a spider mansion and would have never known. All he could focus on was Jared's sad tear-stained face. He looked down at Jared, meeting his warm chocolate eyes before Jared turned away with another sob. Jared heaved in a breath as he wrapped his arms around himself. Self-comforting like he always did.

Husher needed to get through to him.

He needed to prove he was real.

He remained in front of him, an arm's length away, and thought for a second about what to say. It didn't take long for him to pick something stupid enough that Jared was bound to remember.

"Third grade," Husher muttered. "I ate a crayon and when the teacher yelled at me you took a bite of a red crayon and spit it onto her desk—and we had to listen as she explained to the *whole* class how eating crayons was bad."

Jared looked up.

He was still not meeting Husher's eyes, but it was something. Husher thought for a moment it could work and that he might be getting somewhere. However, he knew he needed to make sure he didn't rush it.

As much as he wanted to step forward and drag Jared out of there and run until they were back in the safety of Lones Lake's town square, he knew he needed to let Jared take the step to move closer.

He was getting somewhere so he pushed through. His mind filled with enough random facts about Jared to conjure something up to prove he was real and not some figment of his imagination.

"Your favorite drink is red fruit punch because it stains your tongue and it freaks out the locals, you only listen to 90s country music like a freak." Husher chuckled hopelessly. "And when you try to speak Spanish you still can't roll your r's—"

Husher was cut off when he was practically body-slammed into the wall behind him. For a dizzying moment, he thought a hockey player who was particularly bad at skating on ice had slammed into him as if he were the tempered glass around the rink. Then Jared was wrapping him into a freezing hug that felt like home. He had closed the distance and Husher had a panicking moment that if he so much as blinked, Mason would be rudely waking him up from a dream of his own.

Husher regained his balance and hugged Jared back, the familiarity of it relaxing him. Husher felt like he was going to be sobbing just the same as Jared was a few seconds ago—the only thing keeping him from breaking down was that he knew if he started he wouldn't stop. If he processed any emotions at the moment he was *not* going to be getting out of the house any time soon. He could deal with it later—book a therapy session after everything was over and deal with it then. Even if it felt easier said than done.

He breathed in and Jared smelled too much like the house and not like the apple pie scent he normally smelled like. Husher was still comforted by the cold body hugging him just as desperately. Husher equally clinging to Jared like an anchor.

"Well, that was gayer than the time I realized I liked boobs," Mason chimed in. "You two can kiss later. In the meantime, can we get the fuck out of this creepy-ass house?"

Husher ignored her comments; the urge to never let go of the man in his arms had taken over his mind. He was fully ready to carry the shorter man out of the house if that meant never letting go.

"Mas," Jared whispered. "Shut the fuck up."

Mason smiled and Lee looked just as relieved by the comment.

"Oh, good. It is you, I was concerned for a moment," Mason exclaimed.

Jared pulled back and Husher bit the side of his mouth before he could say something embarrassing. Mason White had too much blackmail on everyone; she did not need anything else.

"Right, let's get out of here then," Lee agreed.

The woman that walked in before Jared opened her mouth and then closed it two times before she spoke. It was like she was trying out for a play as the lead fish or something equally annoying to watch in Husher's mind.

"About that..." the woman trailed off, almost cringing at her own words. "I'm afraid it won't be that easy."

Jared tensed.

"What do you mean?" Husher asked.

Jared rested his head on Husher's shoulder for a moment and Husher was pretty sure if he were a cat he would have been purring at the contact.

"The plants outside that surround the house," Jared sighed. "I can't leave."

"So we fuck em' up," Mason commented. "Break them apart or whatever, right?"

"It's a spell or curse," Jared muttered.

Jared looked around as if someone else was listening to them. "They'll find us."

"If one of them can get out and break the barrier it could work," the unknown woman muttered.

Husher didn't know why they hadn't tried that sooner but figured now was not the right moment to ask anything that could prolong their time there. They needed to get out of that house before anyone found them. The sunlight outside would do nothing to help hide them like it had when they sneaked into the house. They would have to act quickly. The task itself seemed easier said than done. If the house was easy to get out of, Jared *wouldn't* still be there.

Jared turned to the woman. "You said the only way out was to kill Granny. That, yes, the plants were the problem, but after all this time you're now telling me you or Sabrina could have broken the barrier?!"

She backed away. "I tried to get you out the day you showed up. It isn't that easy, they found me *every time* I went to run. I couldn't get caught again."

"So you left us here just like Brandy did—"

"STOP!" The woman covered her mouth as if she just realized how loud she was. "Shit, I'm sorry."

Jared looked at the door and ran over to it before it could open. It took seconds for a hard knock that sounded like the person outside the door wanted to knock it down. Husher met his eyes, wide with horror.

"The window," Jared panicked. "Mas, see if you can climb out and break the barrier, the plants shouldn't bother you."

Husher kept his eyes on Jared who held the door shut while Mason ran over to a broken window. Husher didn't know what to do as he watched in what seemed like slow motion. He rushed over to help Jared keep the door shut when he was met with a meat cleaver rammed into the door, splintering the wood and grazing Jared's arm.

They were out of time, and there was nothing they could do about it. There was no way they would all get out of the window in time. Whoever was on the other side of the door would get into the room; it was no longer a question.

"Uh, my dudes," Mason backed away from the window. "We have another problem."

Husher wished he had friends that didn't end their sentences on cliffhangers and actually said the full information that was needed.

"What is it?!" Husher yelled.

The person on the outside of the door was loudly screaming, though Husher didn't know if it was an unknown language or a mess of nothing.

"There's someone walking back to the house," Mason answered as she reached for her daggers.

They found him, they had gotten there in time, and now it was all falling apart again as Husher watched the door splinter even more, causing Jared to move away from it and in front of his friends.

Jared wasn't safe—none of them were.

A cold hand was pulling him back. Jared was still alive and that had to be enough.

The elderly woman that was chopping in the kitchen stepped closer, her face spilt into a grin Husher would see in his upcoming nightmares. His blood suddenly ran as cold as Jared's, the moment she tilted her decrepit head, he knew they were all fucked.

"Oh, we have guests," she croaked.

Chapter Fifteen
They're Lyin'

Jared Baylor – 27, November (Monday)

"Ew, you fuckass," Mason commented.

It summarized Suzanne Graham rather well.

Granny might have been short, even a little shorter than Jared was—which was saying something—but that meant the pent-up anger had nowhere to go. It was as simple as it was terrifying.

Jared knew the thin door was no match for Granny or the butcher knife she wielded. Even in her old age, she wasn't any less of a threat.

While Jared knew his friends should run, he knew his friends wouldn't leave him. He just needed more time to figure out what to do. Without thinking, when the door broke he moved away from Granny and backed from the only way they could all get out. The window would take too long, as they would need to avoid the already broken glass. Jared knew there wasn't going to be enough time, so he made sure he was in front of his friends. He wasn't going to let them be hurt, especially since he was the reason they were there.

Husher didn't move quick enough and Jared dragged him out of the way, his warm hand oddly comforting in Jared's freezing one. He thought back to Mason's comment, and if they managed to make it out of there he would try and unpack it all then.

Sabrina was the first to move, shocking him and Cheryl both. When Jared looked from Sabrina to Cheryl she seemed to understand what the spawn was going to do before Jared did. The spawn walked over to Granny and hugged her. The simple act wasn't taken lightly even if Jared thought that the moment would have been sweet if it were anyone else. However, it was the Graham family, and there was nothing sweet about them.

Sabrina pushed Granny back out of the doorway as hard as she could. The loud thud and shocked gasp gave them enough time to run.

Cheryl grabbed Sabrina by the arm before running to the side of the house. The screen door was loud as it creaked open, and the breath of fresh air was so close, though the sinking feeling of being trapped was closer.

"Jordan is almost there—we need to go a different way," Cheryl urged.

Jared looked back at Granny. Who had blood on her hand, her knife must have cut her when Sabrina had shoved her. Now, if he could have some more good karma sent his way then he would have no more problems consuming him as he tried to get out of the house and away from the revolting family.

He turned and ran toward the front of the house, dragging Husher along with him. Lee and Mason quickly followed after them.

The door was locked by five different deadbolts as if they had anything valuable inside the house, as if there weren't broken windows and ripped screen doors. Jared was happy he would never understand the Graham family, but it didn't mean there were any fewer questions he had for them.

"Help me unlock them," Jared urged Husher.

He had forgotten he was still holding his hand and quickly let go, leaving the awkward feeling to overthink later. He worked with freeing two of the locks while Husher got the last three by ripping them off the door entirely and throwing them off to the side. When they got the door lock-free it was Mason's turn to get as many of the plants away from the entrance of the house as she could. Jared assumed all they would need is enough room to walk out of the house without touching any of the plants.

Mason ran out with no problem. She looked at the rotting porch without hesitation. Jared thought at the *very* least she would be able to leave and go get help for them, but he hoped things wouldn't come to that. She looked at the plants covering the house and started cutting away through the thick vines and tangled leaves that had many years to plant their own roots. Jared half wanted to laugh at how easy it could have been to get out if he were closer to being human.

Maybe in a few years and after months of therapy sessions, he would be able to laugh at it all. The plants Granny and her husband planted were nothing but waste, ruined by a banshee.

What Jared didn't understand was why a witch actively helped the Graham family protect the house to keep almost any supernatural person out. Maybe it was a joke the witch played on them telling Granny it would keep out any *monster* only for it to keep the supernatural people inside the house until someone broke the spell. Perhaps the witch was just fucking awful at magic.

"The fuck is this shit made of?!" Mason cursed as she cut through one of the bushes.

"Hate," Jared deadpanned.

He could barely see the steps of the porch with how much everything was overgrown. The front of the house must have gotten the most light because it seemed like the place the plants thrived in the most.

Jared knew it wasn't going to be enough time, but it was so close. All they needed was just enough room for them to get out.

There was a loud crash followed by a gunshot.

The thought of people who could barely keep their own balance owning a firearm was not all that comforting. Then again, nothing about the house he was standing in was all that comforting.

The air froze for a moment and the house was silent. Cheryl walked into view, her face blank as the barrel of the shotgun was pointed at her. From the calmness on her face, it most likely wasn't the first time Terry threatened her.

"You invite yourselves into my home and this is how you act, running away, breaking the locks. You should be ashamed," Terry nodded to his own comment.

Jared pushed Lee and Husher behind him as he kept his hands in clear view. He needed to stay calm, but staying calm when all he wanted to do was freak out was not something Jared Baylor was good at.

Quickly, he tried to think of a game plan.

There was no way he could run without getting shot. He didn't know what kind of bullets Terry was using, and given his weakened state he didn't think healing himself would go all that well.

"I was just going to help collect stuff for dinner," Jared lied with gentle ease. "Granny was asking me to help earlier, Cheryl too."

Terry looked at him for a long moment. His eyes felt even more uncomfortable to look at when he was in a mood, the lack of anything behind them were all too eerie. Jared rarely looked people in the eye without cringing back at the uncomfortableness of it and rather faked eye contact, looking between their eyebrows instead, and seemed to be close enough for people not to notice.

"They're lyin'—all of 'em," Granny informed Terry. "The girl was even trying to take poor Sabrina with her. That was their plan. Get into our house, take and take from this family, and take Sabrina with them as if she was theirs!"

Jared could not think of anything worse.

Even if he knew Cheryl wouldn't leave without Sabrina, she wouldn't leave her in the house to rot like the rest of them have already. It was why she was still there years later. Even if she too had begun listening to the family.

Granny was behind it all, in their heads and clawing into their skulls like a brain-eating fungus.

"Ungrateful scum," Terry muttered.

Jared thought about asking Mason for her daggers, but he wasn't all that good at throwing darts, so throwing actual weaponry didn't seem like it would go much better for him. It was almost nice, the feeling of getting out. Him being able to leave and to see the familiar faces of his friends again. He was so close to getting out of there his body ached. The sun shined in through the windows barely touching him, but the orange rays of light painted the broken room into something beautiful. At least in a totally hopeless bottom of the ladder kind of beautiful amongst everything else that seemed so overwhelmingly dark. It was almost amusing that out of everything that was going on around him, the way the sun shined in, painting part of the wall in vibrant color, was the only thing he could focus on in the moment.

Jared knew if he fought back it would end with someone—probably everyone—getting hurt. He didn't have a superhero complex of needing to be the one to save the day; he didn't want to fight anymore.

He just wanted out.

The screen door slammed shut again Jared looked over to see Jordan try and put everything together. His glaze going from Terry then over to Granny, he seemed to put things together quickly when he saw the panicked looks on Jared and his friend's faces.

"So," Mason whispered. "Does this mean we aren't going?"

Terry shot into the air, only hitting the floor to the upstairs and proving to Jared all the more why he wanted to shove the damn gun so far up Terry's ass that it came out his mouth.

Before Jared could tell Husher and Lee to make their way out the door, smoke filled the room much too quickly for it to be anything good. Then again Jared didn't actually know the last time seeing smoke in a house was ever a good thing.

Light footsteps came down the stairs, and for a moment Jared thought it was actually haunted by some old doll in the attic or basement. Perhaps a dummy or child's toy was cursed and had a goal that made everyone in the house suffer. Maybe the place having something *so* haunted trapped there only seemed like it would make sense. Instead, Brandy walked down—which was haunting enough for Jared's liking. The uneasiness was finally settling in and the feeling of giving up felt all too comforting.

Jared tried to look through the thick cloud of smoke that burned from whatever the hell Brandy was holding. He didn't think he would get lucky enough for her to trip down the last step. When she walked into full view, the smell only got worse.

His eyes burned more than the time he was in charge of cutting all the onions for their summer mango salsa at the diner. It wasn't until the smell of mixed herbs burning clued him in on what Brandy was doing.

"Oh, shit," he said in disbelief.

It was Brandy.

She was *the* witch.

Much like Moon, Mason's dad and younger brother, Jared was used to being around a few witches in his life. Most kept to themselves and kept to protection magic, but Brandy was a much different kind of witch.

The burning bundle in her hand was enough to get a choked out cough from Jared. He knew inhaling the smoke would be bad; whatever it was clearly wasn't going to be helpful. Brandy might have been a lot of things, but being helpful was not even close to being one of them. Clearly, though, it didn't much matter what Jared did. The dizziness made him have to focus on not falling as the room felt like he was on a fair ride that was not up to code. It wasn't until he was leaning just a little too far that he even realized he was falling, the room filled with a smoky haze he could do nothing about. He knew he should have hit the floor, but the impact of it never came.

He tried to talk. He even tried to move, but his body wouldn't listen to him. He closed his eyes for a second too long. He just needed a moment, and then he could help get his friends out of there.

It would be fine; he had to get them out.

He looked up and saw Husher fall beside him. Jared tried to move but he couldn't, and in that moment he wished he had died. At least then his friends wouldn't have been stuck there because of him.

Chapter Sixteen
Don't Moisturize with Poison Ivy

Husher Carden – 28, November (Tuesday)

For a long moment, Husher thought he had dreamt it all. It wouldn't have been the first time his subconscious decided to create a detailed dream so realistic like all the times he woke up having to come to terms with that he could not in fact fly or live in a little mushroom house.

Though this time he would have killed for the fantasy of living in a little mushroom house again.

This dream felt more like the times he would fall asleep watching a play-through of one of the popular animated horror games he liked. It was like no matter where the character in the game went they were met with another villain wanting to kill them and their health was only a quarter of the way filled.

Instead, he was met with the cold darkness around him that felt too much like reality for his liking.

The last thing he remembered was passing out. He had tried his best to catch Jared and Lee, but he wasn't sure he managed to catch either one of them before he was falling to the ground himself.

Husher looked around for a moment, but the only lighting was from a candle on what looked like a butcher block counter covered in wax. He was tied to a chair rope laced with what smelled like wild basil. The old myth of werewolves being allergic to wild basil was ridiculous—pure wild basil-infused oil apparently acted like an irritating allergy.

It felt like he just moisturized with poison ivy.

He thought he was going to be sick.

Husher knew the trip out into the middle of fucking nowhere was not going to end well. He didn't know just *how* bad it was going to be. He should have known that everything that had happened however many hours ago—was going to end in some crappy situation.

He knew the house was the embodiment of *bad vibes,* when they first arrived, but being drugged and trapped in what looked like a basement was not what he had in mind. His backpack uncomfortably dug into his back that was haphazardly pressed to the back of the chair he was tied to.

He let his eyes glow, taking in the room around him.

The space was smaller than he thought, and at least he wasn't alone.

Lee was to his right tied to a chair as well, Jared to his left, and the raven-haired woman across from him. It was like they were all in a circle, Mason being the only one missing. Husher hoped she got away and would get help. She was outside when the person drugged them. The smoke might not have gotten to her—not to mention banshees were as close to humans as they got. There wasn't any herb from the eighteen hundreds that would harm her any more than it would a human. She would have been fine as long as she was able to get away from the commotion that Husher was still unsure that he didn't just imagine it.

When he scanned the room there was slight movement, the unknown woman blinked awake, as she slowly looked around the room, he quickly switched his eyes back to normal so he didn't get caught.

"Hey," Husher whispered. "Where are we?"

He didn't know if she had been taken like them, but given she had a gun to her head the last Husher saw, it was a good guess she would be willing to talk at the very least.

"Basement," she muttered.

She shouldn't have been affected by the smoke, at least Husher didn't think she would have been. She seemed human. Then again, they might have given her something else or hit her in the head to knock her out. It seemed fitting for them.

"Are we alone or do you think they're coming back?" Husher whispered.

Husher didn't know how long he had been out. It felt like the times he took a nap in the middle of an afternoon and woke up to the sun completely set and his bedroom fully immersed into the dark. It was a dreadful and confusing feeling that seemed like he had somehow entered another universe in the span of a few hours. It was never as long of a time as he thought, usually only a few hours at most. Being unconscious, though, made a few minutes feel like hours, and a few minutes could end up being a few days. With no windows in sight, it was difficult to tell what time it was.

"I think," she started. Her voice was shaky, most likely due to being knocked out. "They most likely let us sleep off the drugs. They'll be back at some point."

Husher half rolled his eyes. "That isn't comforting."

He suspected as much, but what bothered him was their motive. Not knowing what would happen when they found out they were waking up was also high on that list of questions he wasn't sure he wanted to know the answer to.

"Can't say any of this is all that comforting," Lee's voice made him jump a little.

When he turned to them it was useless to see if they were okay; all he could see wasn't much more than their shadow with his regular vision.

"Where are we anyway? This place looks much like a horror plot—and I know I'm white, but I'm not this level of white to end up in the basement," Lee grumbled.

Which, to be fair, it really did look like a haunted house that some—most likely white—person—who would be too curious about something haunted and just walk right into it as if they were invited. No matter the trespassing signs and people telling them it's a bad idea. It was like going to hide in the garage full of chainsaws instead of getting into the running car.

Husher didn't know why or how people didn't just understand it was a good rule of thumb to leave things like abandoned houses or creepy dolls alone. Anything that looks haunted, leave it be. Simple, really.

Apparently not for everyone.

Husher would have to talk to Jared about it later because if they did manage to get out of there he did not want the brunet repeating any of this.

"Feels like one too," the stranger muttered. "I've been here for years—and it doesn't get any more comforting."

Husher wanted to ask how anyone could manage hat

"You're the babysitter," Lee muttered. "Cheryl Ward right, the one that went missing for five years?" Apparently, Lee was wasting no time in asking.

Husher had no idea where Lee got the energy from; they were just as asleep as he had been moments ago. Lee was talking normally while Husher still felt like there was more gauze in his mouth than when he had his wisdom teeth ripped out. He tried not to question it and listened for an answer. However, he was met with a soft chuckle or choked-out sob instead he wasn't all that sure. Leaving the room dead silent for a moment too long for his liking before the stranger finally answered.

Husher was hit by the thought that maybe she hadn't realized it had been that long. Hell, Husher was sure he had only been there for a few hours, but the time didn't pass like it normally did. If he was here for years he would have lost track. He wondered if Jared knew how long he had been missing.

"Yeah, I am," Cheryl answered.

"And you're the only other person they took—other than Jared?" Husher asked.

"As long as I've been here, yes, but there were some they attempted to take before scaring them off the property," she answered bluntly.

Husher still had no idea how no one had found out about the house. Someone from the town would have eventually come to sell it or do something with the property while it was still in its better years. Before it rotted away to whatever mess it currently was.

"I used to babysit Sabrina when I was sixteen." She chuckled, more hollow and broken than anything else. "I knew the family was weird, knew that I didn't like being here too late, but after a while I just couldn't leave her here with them."

"So you decided to stay here?" Lee questioned.

"They wouldn't let me leave one night. I just thought they knew I was going to call CPS on them and try to get Sabrina out of these living conditions," Cheryl confessed.

"Then why not just sneak out in the middle of the night?" Husher couldn't help but ask. He assumed she had tried before, but he had to ask. Husher didn't quite know how she was stuck there, but then again, she was clearly attached to the creepy kid from earlier, so he wasn't all that sure what to think of her choices.

"I had!" Cheryl exclaimed. "I even called for help, but the authorities thought it was a joke and Brandy—the mom—found my phone and thought I was trying to have their location found or something."

Husher was not comforted by that either.

Even if he knew where his backpack was, his phone no doubt wouldn't work out this far into the woods. Though he knew his first call would be to his parents over the authorities. With the way the day was going, he would be stuck with Joel, who would think it was a prank as well.

"Now, I just know too much for them to let me go without killing me," Cheryl added blankly.

Husher nodded, knowing full well no one saw him. It was out of habit at his point.

"They sell shit from the field behind the house," Jared muttered.

At the sound of his voice, Husher nearly gave himself whiplash turning in Jared's direction. Husher went to check, but the rope digging into his wrists reminded him that he was still tied to the chair. Moving would only make his arms itch even worse from the oil they soaked the rope with, and he didn't want to make the healing process any worse than it would be.

"If I could slap you and hug you right now I would," Lee muttered.

Husher shook his head. "I think what they mean is, what the fuck, Jared? How was this a quick walk?!"

"No, I still kinda wanna slap him," Lee corrected.

"Wow, thanks," he muttered, pausing for a moment before continuing. "I just started thinking about some things, then when I looked up, I didn't know where I was. I didn't even know I walked into the woods or off the path… I just kinda got lost and then I saw a house."

"So you just walked right in?!" Husher whispered in disbelief.

"What, no?!" Jared remarked. "I'm not a total dumbass!"

"The pickup guy found him," Cheryl muttered. "Thought he was going to bust their little business."

"I didn't mean to," Jared whispered low enough that Husher thought he imagined it at first.

Husher was not going to stay there any longer nor was he going to let anyone else have to stay there either.

Depending on how long it had been, his parents would be waking up soon. They would find his note, they would know where to find him, and Husher knew they would make the authorities look like kindergartners when they found the house.

They just needed to figure out how to get out of the basement.

He knew if they got out of there they could make a run for it, maybe even draw the family's attention somewhere else. Knowing the field would be the focus, it seemed like they would be easy enough to trick.

Husher took a shallow breath.

He knew Jared and Lee were safe at least. Mason could have also gotten out and gone for backup.

They would have to get themselves out of the basement somehow—then hopefully help would find them before the creepy family did.

Chapter Seventeen
Let it go up in Flames

Jared Baylor – 28, November (Tuesday)

J ared thought for a moment he could get loose, but his wrists were tied too tight and it felt too much like a losing battle. He felt like he was drained, sleeping too much for one day and there was no energy to begin with.

"We just need to get out of the basement," Husher said in a low voice. "Then we'll deal with the rest."

"Oh, I planned on sitting here all week," Lee deadpanned.

Before Jared could say anything the all too familiar sound of creaking floorboards made him pause for a moment. Listening to the sounds above them, walking closer and closer to the basement door until he heard it open loudly, breaking the silence around them.

Jared listened, trying to figure out who it was by the sound alone, but was unsuccessful. He didn't know if his brain was playing tricks on him or if he was still out of it from his surprise nap. He tried to look over to Cheryl, not being able to see anything more than a vague silhouette of where he heard her talking; however, he doubted she would be any more tense than she was before. The confusion turned into dread as he heard another set of footsteps and another that he recognized as Sabrina's. When the three figures came into sight bringing a flashlight with them, Jared thought he could have floated in the air due to the weight lifted off his chest.

Then he couldn't see anything for a moment but the bright blinding light as it rushed across him and landed right in his face. If he had woken up a few minutes later, he would have been way more concerned about seeing a bright white light.

"Mas, could you not do that," Jared groaned.

Mason moved the flashlight off of his face and onto her next victim as Jared tried to blink away the LED lights that appeared every time he closed his eyes. When he was finally able to see again, he saw the raw confused relief wash over Cheryl.

Mason grinned at them. "Have a good nap?"

"Let's just say if I could give you the finger right now—" Jared paused for effect, "I would."

"Fair," Mason shrugged before hitting Jordan over the head. Jared didn't even notice him standing there—which to be fair, he couldn't see for a good minute—but he thought he would have smelled the dude at least. Maybe his sense of smell was going to shit too from being stuck there for so long. The smell of fresh laundry or soap felt like a pipe dream at this point.

"Untie them," Mason ordered.

Jared looked over to Cheryl again. As if Jordan would listen to anyone, even Granny sometimes couldn't get through to him. Yet, in the dim lighting, Jared saw a look of fear on his face. It was always impressive and terrifying when Mason White was in charge.

"I wanna help too." Sabrina smiled, stepping into view.

Mason looked back for a moment, finding a discarded hunting blade on the workbench behind her. Jared knew before it was too late what Mason was thinking. Without thought, Mason carefully handed over the knife to Sabrina and gave the spawn a thumbs up. "Only cut the ropes, not the people," Mason reminded her.

Sabrina nodded and rushed over to Cheryl first, somehow not stabbing anyone in the process, and cut the ropes. Jordan cut the rest of their ropes before suddenly being rather unsure of himself and finding the floor extremely interesting. It was the most silent Jared had ever seen him.

Jared looked at his wrists burned by the rope, but it was nothing that wouldn't heal once he drank something. Currently, it felt like he had drunk a glass of sandpaper, since it had been so long since he last had blood or anything that wasn't rotting. It was just another thing he would have to deal with later. At the moment he just had to ignore all the heartbeats in the room; he was used to never acting on the urges to sink his fangs in a wrist or something. Feeding from the vein had always seemed kinda creepy to him and was not something he ever planned on doing. It would just be another thing the townspeople would gossip about until he was thrown out of town for a crime he didn't commit. He was perfectly fine drinking the bottled blood if it meant keeping his own sanity.

"When we get out of here, you're telling me what you did to make him so scared of you," Jared muttered to Mason.

"Why wait." She gave a smirk that was far from comforting. "I just sang a little *song.*"

Jared cringed the moment she said it. His ears hurt just at the thought of her using her scream to sing, the melodic spell was almost a deafening sound that would no doubt still be ringing in Jordan's ears for the next week. He was suddenly very grateful to have been passed the fuck out and not conscious enough to hear that.

Jared nodded. "Yeah, that will do it."

Cheryl looked around then back up to the steps, confused and hesitant to ask something. Lee, on the other hand, didn't care as they walked over to the steps, only pausing a moment to turn toward Mason and ask what they all wanted to know.

"So the others..." Lee trailed off a bit. "Where are they?"

Jared looked over to Mason for the answer as well. There was no way she could have taken them all down alone. Sure, she was a skilled fighter, going to boxing matches every once in a while and being the reason the garage she works at no longer got robbed since then. But Mason had not met a truly unsettling family like the Grahams. They were like their own disease or insect that no matter how much you tried to treat always came back stronger. It felt too much like the times in the autumn and spring when stink bugs would overtake his windows and he would be stuck picking them off his plants before they had a chance to destroy his leafy children.

However, Mason was Mason, and Jared should have expected nothing less than when people were violent she was worse.

"Stabbed the one bitch," she sighed. "Shitlord was hit in the head with a frying pan when he tried to shoot me. The old bitch, I have no idea where she went, and my buddy over there was reminded to be grateful for his ability to hear—just maybe in a few hours. I don't think it's all returned yet."

"We can leave?" Cheryl whispered in disbelief.

"Well, I'm sure as fuck not going to make you stay," Mason informed her.

A silence fell upon them.

Jared was still questioning how it was even real. Living there for the past few months, he was hesitant to believe something as satisfactory as being able to leave—it all felt too good to be true. He couldn't begin to understand how Cheryl felt after years of being there.

Apparently, though, Cheryl took the news much better than Jared was expecting.

She was the first upstairs, Jared and his friends moving out of her way and following after her. Jared knew that they didn't need Terry waking up from his hit in the head or Brandy waking up from her stab wound—okay, maybe he wanted her to wake up and just be too stabbed to do anything about them leaving. He didn't want to be linked to a murder. He just wasn't sure what to expect when he walked upstairs. Mason must have noticed, because she had bumped him in the shoulder to get his attention

"Stop that look. I didn't kill anyone," she informed him.

The comment was *not* as comforting as he hoped.

Once upstairs, it still left the question as to where Granny was.

Jared watched Cheryl look at the unconscious couple tied to the dining room chairs. Terry with his head bent forward and a bruise forming on the side of his face, while Brandy's arm was wrapped around the kitchen knife embedded into it.

"Okay," Cheryl nodded. "Sabrina, grab *Mx. One Eye* and whatever else you want to take with you."

Sabrina nodded and rushed off to her playroom to most likely grab her concerning stuffed animals. If they got out of there, he hoped Cheryl would be able to get the spawn a copy of *Frankenstein.* It seemed fitting for her.

Meanwhile, Cheryl wasted no time walking out to the garage. It was like something had been switched now that she was able to get out with Sabrina without anyone stopping her. Jared watched with concern when she returned with an old gas can. It might have been years since the family left the house; however, Jared always noticed gas cans were full out in the garage. Most likely the field behind the house was on some kind of timer thanks to the person who came to pick up the product. They must've also been the ones to refill the gas cans, though Jared still had no idea why there would have been electricity—or anything from the past few decades—out there and not in the house.

Then again Granny might have been the cause of it. For all Jared knew, Granny didn't even know what was behind the house. She only went to the backyard but the rotting fence would have been enough to block her view.

"We need to leave," Lee spoke.

Husher took Jared by the hand and dragged him to the door. A door Jared had tried to get out before and failed way too many times.

It was like an invisible bubble that kept him stuck.

This time was different, and not because he was being tugged outside but because he was actually going outside. Out into the darkness of morning or night, his brain was too mushy to notice which way the sun was coming from to tell what time of day it was.

He was out.

Actually outside.

Finally, he could breathe. After a few seconds of fresh air and peace with no weight on his chest, it was like he was sixteen again and sleeping in Moon's apartment above the diner. The couch that was turned into a makeshift bed had felt like freedom that night.

Now he felt the same rush of adrenaline.

He was out of there, Lee and Mason were safe and Husher was there clutching onto his hand with the same grasp Jared had, neither wanting to let go in case it actually was a dream. They were not wanting to wake up when this seemed to be working out for them.

Then Cheryl walked out with Sabrina, and Jordan was looking back in panic, the yelling made everything feel real again. Jared didn't know if Jordan was yelling because he still couldn't hear or if he was just trying to get everyone's attention.

"She's fucking crazy!" he screamed.

Jared stared blankly at him.

He didn't care for anyone being called that after years of his parents being called *'crazy'* or *'insane'* when they were failed by a system that was broken from the start. Words like that only added to the things he had normalized as a kid only to learn later that those were not things he should have thought as *'normal'* or even okay. It wasn't until Jared made friends that he even noticed what real affection and respect were. Even after cutting his parents out of his life he still didn't appreciate such an ignorant sentence. Too many nights were spent thinking about how his parents could have been if they had friends like Jared did. If they were shown kindness instead.

Cheryl laughed. "I say we burn the shit hole down."

Jared suddenly clued in on why she grabbed the gas and why it took her so long to come out of the house. And Jordan's screaming made much more sense.

"You can't kill anyone!" Jared yelled to her.

Cheryl shook her head. "Okay, close your eyes and put your fingers in your ears."

Jared tried to rush over to stop her, but Husher pulled him back. "You are not helping her kill anyone!" He would just have to settle for yelling and hoping for the best. "You won't get Sabrina if they learn you did this."

It was enough for her to pause.

She looked down at the girl by her side, the reason she was stuck there to begin with. Jordan was still standing by her, looking up at the house only to back away from it as if he suddenly saw a ghost. He turned to Cheryl, grabbing the flip lighter she had in her hand.

"I'll do it!" Jordan exclaimed.

Jared was not expecting him to change his mind so quickly, but when he looked back to the house, he saw the silhouette of Granny. He understood the quick change of heart the best he could.

Cheryl nodded and grabbed Sabrina before she started running.

In a matter of seconds, Jared watched the house go up in flames.

Fire rushed into the house just as quickly as the thick gray smoke came rushing out of the open door and broken windows. The house was burning and in it were three people Jared thought finally got their share of karma, though he wasn't quite sure this was what he had meant when he originally wished for the family to get the hell they dished out in return.

Jordan ran away from the bright flames—the house that harmed too many, and the house no one was sorry to see burn away. At least, the temperature of the fire helped warm his skin as he probably stood too close for anyone's comfort.

When Jared stared too long, unmoving, Husher grabbed him, threw him over his shoulder, and started running for the woods. Jared was still in too much shock to comment about being manhandled.

He was fucking free.

Chapter Eighteen
Lost in the Woods Equals Piggyback Rides

Husher Carden – 28, November (Tuesday)

"Put me down!" Jared yelled, hitting Husher on the back as he ran.

Husher had no idea why he was still carrying Jared. Husher had panicked when he noticed Jared wasn't running and grabbed him before either of them got stuck in the fire.

They were in the woods and Husher sincerely hoped Lee remembered the way out of there, because Husher felt as lost as Jared usually did. Husher stopped and put Jared down a little more gracefully than he had thrown him over his shoulder like a sack of potatoes. Husher rolled his shoulder before relaxing it. In hindsight, he probably should have thought it through first. Jared didn't care to be touched unless he was the one to initiate it, much like a cat.

Husher waited to be hit again, but it never came. Instead, chocolate eyes were settled on him with an unreadable stare. Husher didn't know if he should apologize or drag him along again, because if they didn't keep moving, they would be lost.

"Stop staring at me!" Jared yelled.

And there he was.

"You're the one sta—not the time. Let's go!" Husher cut himself off; now was clearly not the time to unpack whatever *that* was.

Husher took Jared by the wrist and pulled him along. They had not come all this way just to get caught up in the fire.

They caught up with the others quickly, following the path they had used before. Running probably wasn't totally necessary at that point. The house was out of sight and lost in the November trees. The only sign there was something wrong was the smoke creating gray clouds in the sky. However, he didn't want to take any chances even though Husher knew he probably should have been more concerned about the three people that were most likely burnt to death just a few minutes ago or who were still burning. He didn't know how long it took for people to burn in a house fire and was definitely not going to look it up.

He knew he should have probably tried to stop them like Jared had attempted to do.

He knew it would have been the right thing to do, but they were people who had tried to kill him and his friends, the repulsive beings that had trapped people—that he knew of—in living conditions no one should have been in, so the basic empathy he normally had vanished quickly.

The sun had set by the time they made it to the halfway point in the woods. The dark sky helped as much as it had when they first walked the path. Husher had no idea what time it was or where they were. Looking forward, Lee's eyebrows furrowed as they looked around. Husher felt just as confused as they looked.

"Shit!" Cheryl tripped over the uneven ground. She had managed to run most of the way with the kid on her back.

When they took a moment to pause it gave Lee enough time to look around, though Husher wasn't sure what good it would do considering they wouldn't be able to see too far into the distance even with flashlights. Husher thought the area looked familiar, but the entire woods looked the same to him. Everything still smelled off since being in that house. The fresh air was not as helpful with finding an old scent and using it as a way out of the woods.

"I think we went this way, right?" Lee informed them, even though it came off more like a question.

Mason waved a dagger around. "Yep, it was *definitely* that way."

Husher looked at the path they just came from and the one Mason was pointing at with one of her twin daggers. They both looked the same, one with less travel down to it but with the same dead plants and jagged weeds over-ground to the point even the muddy path looked nonexistent. It was anyone's guess at that point. Picking a path that would most likely get them lost again or still since Husher remained a bit unsure where they were.

"Okay, so I guess we just keep going?" Lee asked.

"Well, I'm not going back," Jared chimed in.

Husher forgot he was still holding his wrist and quickly let go while waiting for the others to figure out what direction they would choose, hoping they wouldn't ask him.

If they kept walking in one direction they were bound to make it out at some point, probably.

By the time they were able to start running again, Husher was given Sabrina to carry the rest of the way, a task he was not thrilled about but complied with anyway. Cheryl looked like she could barely get herself out of the woods, and Sabrina's bare feet were vulnerable to the many thorny vines so close to the ground. Husher cringed at the thought of someone having to walk on the ground without shoes, it would have been like walking on needles. Even with shoes the path wasn't all that pleasant.

It was taking them longer to get out of there than it had to find the house, or at least to Husher it seemed that way. The rush of adrenaline or the buzzing energy the full moon gave him might have contributed to the feeling. In their panic they must have made a wrong turn at some point on their way out. That ultimately might have played into the time. It had gotten to the point where even Jared thought they were walking in circles, which Husher knew was bad.

Mason was leading, cutting any plant that got in her way, and everyone kept their distance just in case. It seemed to go quicker when she was in the lead and clearing away most of the brush near the path. Husher at least didn't have to deal with too many thorns catching on his pant legs anymore.

"Great night to be stuck in the woods," Jordan grumbled. He had been silent for most of the walk like the rest of them. All of them were too busy running the hell out of there and trying to get back into their hometown to actually care about talking.

"Better than Granny's dinner," Cheryl snapped.

Husher tuned it out after that, focusing on making sure everyone was still there and that Mason didn't get out of sight before they could catch up with her. However, at the thought, she paused for a moment as he watched the weapons in the air as she slashed through a vine, twin daggers were probably not meant for such a task, but it managed to cut the vine with ease.

Husher looked up as he walked closer to her, wondering why after nearly running ahead the whole time Mason had stopped so suddenly. And when Husher saw the reason—a person up ahead—he grew cold.

Things only grew worse when he listened to the whispers behind him.

"That's him," Cheryl whispered.

"Who?" Lee asked, unable to see until they walked closer.

"Pickup," Sabrina answered for them. The kid's voice was about as comforting as her smile, but it was an answer, nonetheless.

It wasn't all that helpful for Husher, but the tone of voice and Jordan becoming eerily still, had to click that whatever it was, it was *not* good. Husher knew a few things about Joel Smith. He knew what the town gossip said about him and he knew he didn't trust the man any more than he trusted hammock swings. Running into him in the middle of the woods after the night they had just sent a shiver down his spine rather than giving him any hope. There was some instinct that Husher picked up on, his inner beta warning him about something.

The uncomfortable feeling in his stomach was never good news.

"Fuck," Jared whispered. It was low enough that Husher barely heard it but enough to confirm this wasn't right. There was something off about the whole thing.

"Well, well," Joel muttered, like the smartass he was—then again, that would imply to some degree he was smart. Husher knew damn well the man was dumber than a fly on a trap.

For a long moment, Husher had thought back to when they were out looking for Jared and how badly he wanted to punch the smirk off Joel's face after hearing the comments he was making. The same urge struck him again. Husher had never punched anyone and he knew it wouldn't end well for him, but at that moment he didn't really care about the consequences. However, he was still stuck carrying Sabrina, and if he wanted to put her down Joel would see the punch coming, so he wouldn't be able to land it somewhere along his much too punchable face.

"So, what are y'all doing out here?" Joel asked.

Husher looked at him for a moment unsure of what to do. Sure, they could tell the truth, but something told Husher that Joel wasn't there as a deputy.

Mason, on the other hand, didn't seem to care.

"Oh, so you don't know yet?" she laughed. "Look up."

Husher watched the cocky smile on Joel's face disappear as he just then seemed to notice the dark sky tinted gray. Husher was sure they would be able to see it better when they managed to get out of the thick trees, but it was enough to notice there was something in the distance.

"What have you done?" Joel gritted out, looking back at them no longer the happy deputy who did no wrong.

Mason slowly backed away before she flipped him off and started running again. Husher looked at her wide-eyed before quickly following suit and ignored the booming voice behind them.

"You're all fucking dead!" Joel seethed.

Husher ducked behind trees as he ran deeper into the woods, ignoring the path altogether as he tried his best not to trip. The dark and uneven rocky terrain made him feel all too much like a main character being chased in a movie where the characters of course panicked, ultimately being slashed to death by the killer. It wasn't the best thing to think about while he was trying to avoid becoming one of those people.

Husher did his best to keep his balance, coming close to falling when his foot connected with a stuck-out rock and almost pushed him forward. He caught himself. Jared, on the other hand, wasn't as lucky when his foot hit the same rock.

Husher stopped and turned back, making sure Jared could get up. Any other time he wouldn't have worried, but with his weakened state Husher wasn't going to take any chances. It would have been easy for him to have twisted an ankle or broken something.

"You guys need to keep moving!" Mason yelled.

She ran back over, taking her backpack off and putting it on backwards before taking Sabrina and putting the kid on her back before she began running again. Husher would question where she got the energy later and in the meantime, he turned to Jared and hoped he wouldn't be as stubborn, as he usually was.

Husher helped Jared up and took off his backpack, handing it over to him. Jared looked confused but put it on anyway.

Husher turned around and crouched down as Mason had with Sabrina.

Sabrina had been more of an adult about the situation, meanwhile it took two seconds for Jared to turn into the temperamental child he was deep down.

"No," Jared muttered stubbornly. "I am not getting a damn piggyback ride."

It was wishful thinking Jared wouldn't be a bit stubborn about it, but Mason was getting too far ahead and it would be much quicker if Husher just carried him.

"Jared Lucas Baylor, get on my damn back or I'll throw you over my shoulder again," Husher stated firmly.

A moment of silence passed, a few seconds that gave Husher the answer he needed. He didn't have to be facing him to know the pouted glare that was on his best friend's face. The same glare that meant Husher had won but Jared wasn't happy about it. Jared grumbled something under his breath before he climbed onto Husher's back, holding onto his shoulders as Husher held onto Jared's thighs, wrapping them around his torso the best he could before running again.

"I am never going to live this down, am I?" Jared groaned.

"I don't think *anything* about this is going to be forgotten quickly," Husher informed him.

They were all out of breath by the time they realized they had lost Joel. Husher assumed he most likely rushed to the house in a panic so he could see whatever was left of the house and whatever it was that he was helping the family sell.

Husher hoped it was all gone.

The realization of everything had yet to set in about the evening or even the last however many hours, but Husher knew that when it did, it would hit him full force.

Chapter Nineteen
Autumn Leaves This Time of Year

Jared Baylor – 28, November (Tuesday)

While the air smelled crisper, he knew it most likely was just because he escaped from a house that smelled like rotting flesh on a good day. He was just glad not to have experienced that house in the summer.

When they made it out of the woods, Husher stopped running.

Jared knew Joel would be back and even worse to deal with now that they had pissed him off, but they had lost him long enough to stop running and catch their breath. Jared would have felt bad for letting Husher carry him, mortified even at how unawkward it was, but he was too tired to care. Husher knew he had failed P.E. because he refused to run. It was like being hit with whiplash when he accidentally used his vampire speed. He hated it—he hated how he was always sweaty and the gym uniform always clung to him and made the feeling worse somehow.

"Wow, they hung the lights up?" Cheryl more or less asked.

Jared paused his memories of how depressing his high school years were, noticing the streets of Lones Lake were lit up with string lights for the holidays as they were every year from the middle of November through the first week of January.

It helped make it through the sometimes gloomy winter.

"Yeah, almost a week ago," Lee informed her.

It was comforting to see the familiar lights, but it also made Jared realize just how homesick he was. How the approaching winter air felt on his dirty and greasy skin. Getting a shower could not come soon enough.

The air felt freeing around him even if it did little to help his mobility. Jared wrapped his legs a bit tighter around Husher's waist, he was so close to using the blond's shoulder as a pillow. It was unfair how warm Husher ran compared to Jared. He took a moment and breathed in, and shit if it didn't feel like home. A place that Jared truly didn't think he would be quite as happy to see again, as he was.

He looked up, noticing the autumn leaves decorating the grass and a bit of the sidewalk. It made him miss the place more than he would have ever thought, a hint of nostalgia he hadn't expected. He almost felt like he was dreaming or maybe it felt more like a broken memory his brain gave him due to a lack of food. He didn't know if he cared all that much.

Then warm arms were still holding him up, steady and painfully dependable. It was real, he knew that. He knew the world around him didn't just pause even if it genuinely felt like that.

He took another breath and let it out slower.

The houses that already had their winter lights up, too early and taken down too late to say which holidays they were even up for. All of them, some of them, none of them, Jared didn't really care. He remembered watching people so panicked about getting their lights up before the first snow of the year.

The familiar places were are all decorated with colorful, bright, and sometimes twinkling lights. It all looked prettier than he remembered. Usually, he groaned at the thought of the rush of customers, the bad carolers, and the even worse movies—but the familiarity was comforting.

"You good?" Husher asked.

"Yeah..." Jared trailed off. Seeing familiar places he had seen for years and with shiny decorations up only made it all the more overwhelming. "It's just a bit much."

Husher nodded and Jared left it at that. He couldn't tell him why he even went for the damn walk in the first place and that after being in the house for the first month he had nearly given up on getting out and living again.

Jared let Husher carry him to the police station. They all seemed to silently agree it was better to get ahead of the whole Joel thing—and the burning down a house thing—and the fact the house might have had three people still inside. Jared wasn't all that sure how he expected it to go.

"I don't know why we have to do this," Jordan muttered.

Jordan had been silent most of the run and Jared wasn't sure how to react to the person who punched him in the face just because he was in the same room, then like a switch helping burn the house down with Granny still inside. It didn't make any sense—then again, Jared didn't know how he would be if he didn't have his loved ones. Jordan lacked that comfort, and while it didn't excuse his behavior, it was still something Jared had to consider.

"Because you burned down a house and two of us were missing," Jared stated.

He tapped the blond on the shoulder to put him down, it took Husher a moment to understand what he meant.

"Oh, right," he crouched down and let go.

The town around him seemed to spin for a moment, but he ignored it.

He was fine.

They just needed to go inside the station and things would be figured out, and he would be able to go to sleep in his own bed with more pillows than necessary and fluffy blankets he could bury himself under as soon as he got home—well, maybe a shower first.

It didn't actually matter when in a few minutes it all shattered when he saw a car speeding in his direction. Joel booking it back in record time, throwing his car in park while Jared watched him slam the car door

Luckily—or unluckily—Jared was nearly in the door of the station the moment Joel nearly hit them with his car.

Mason smirked and pointed to the camera at the front of the station.

Lee had their phone in hand recording it all hopefully.

Jared smiled the awkward way white people did when they passed someone on the street, just a flat line of ac-knowledgement.

He pulled the door open and ushered everyone in quickly. If they got Samuel or literally anyone other than—

The door opened and Joel stormed in with his worst half—or rather his partner from Hell.

Jared wasn't sure why, but every time he saw the woman on Joel's right he felt an instant headache. He only knew Stephanie Fisher from the haircare store and he always kinda hated when she was the one ringing things up. He didn't understand how someone who worked in a place like that could have such damaged, over-bleached, and un-toned hair.

It didn't take long for the sheriff to walk out of his office, and Jared didn't know if it was the noise of the door or the strong perfume odor coming from Stephanie that had lured him out with a frown. Maybe it was just all the commotion in the middle of his station.

"Oh, good," Stephanie started as she walked over to Samuel pointing a finger at him. Jared wondered if twen-ty-eight was old enough to qualify her to be a Karen or not.

Samuel looked up, seeing everyone who was dragging mud into the station, then over to Joel as if to ask what was going on. He was much calmer than Jared would have been in his situation.

The door burst open again, and Moon and Husher's moms rushed in.

Jared really didn't give a shit and melted into the hug from Moon, instantly comforted by the familiar feeling. Warm arms wrapped around him as he inhaled the mix of herbs she always smelled like. He entirely forgot that he was covered in mud from his fall in the woods earlier—and not showering since he had gone missing was probably worse smelling than Stephanie's personality.

"How did you know we were here so fast?" Husher asked, confused.

"Mrs. Bell said she saw you walking into town," Nicole answered.

Stephanie cut in. "I just think you should know. There is a fire!" she shouted above the crowd now forming in the lobby of the police station.

Jared wondered how the woman learned about the fire so quickly, then it dawned on him that if Joel was helping sell the product with the Graham family then there was a chance that Stephanie was the blonde Cheryl was talking about being someone never to meet.

The shoe fit, but Jared didn't want to touch it. Part of him hoped this would be a good time for him to be wrong about something. He just wasn't all that optimistic about it.

"You do realize this isn't the fire station, right? You should call—" Mason began but was cut off.

"These monsters were the ones behind it. Burning down a house is a crime, you know," Stephanie crossed her arms.

Moon raised a brow at the woman. Jared could hear it coming before Moon was speaking up. "Really, what about stealing from your place of employment? And for what, broken bleached hair with that apricot complexion? Honey, just shut the fuck up."

Jared wanted to laugh at how quickly Stephanie shut up. Maybe he did laugh—he didn't actually know nor did he care at the moment.

"Okay, I'll take this group in for questioning. Someone get the information on the fire and let the fire department know about it immediately!" Samuel shouted to one of the newer deputies. "As for anyone else, wait here and I will be back to talk with you all unless anyone else wants to add anything crucial. Now would be the time." He waited a moment before nodding at the lack of response. "Great."

He gestured for Jared and his friends—plus Jordan and Sabrina—to follow him down the hall.

Jared might have zoned out a bit since he had no idea that the tiny building could even have a room for questioning. He just thought they would be led to an office in the back or something. However, that was not the case, and there was a proper two-way mirror in the room along with a table with a thin layer of dust on the top of it. He didn't have much to compare it to other than a few crime movies. It was a low-crime town, and he was pretty sure this was the first time the room had been used in years.

"I will be questioning you separately," Samuel informed them.

Jared just nodded along, not really paying much attention to anything.

It felt like seconds passed waiting in the hall for it to be his turn, which he knew wasn't true, he was busy zoning out as he looked at the few marks on the floor.

Once he was in the room, he wasn't even sure what he was saying. He knew who took him but wasn't able to tell him that much; his brain wasn't working. Everything around him felt like he was walking into a thunderstorm on a foggy day.

The sheriff was talking, but Jared had no idea what he was saying.

"Jared?" Lee snapped their fingers in his face, but he must not have reacted as much as he thought. He wasn't even sure when Lee had gotten there. It felt like his body wasn't really there when he moved. He couldn't feel anything and vaguely heard whispers of if he was *okay* or if he was *dying*—that one seemed a bit dramatic.

"Here," he was handed something, but when he reached for the bottle his arm was too cold. He just needed to warm up, then he could take the bottle. Instead, the bottle was held close and he felt rough hands on his face. When the drink hit his tongue it was all-consuming, as if the world was put back into focus after being blurred for so long. When he could move again he took the bottle and finished it before he noticed the chicken wrap placed in front of him.

He looked up and the sheriff nodded. Jared quickly ate, trying to ignore his fangs still being out. He had been so hungry he couldn't get them to go back in at the moment and had to deal with chewing and not biting himself in his rush.

His senses seemed to heighten, or he had been too out of his own head before eating to notice all the sounds in the room.

The light over the table created a frustrating buzzing noise, the sound of himself chewing, the heartbeats of everyone in the room with him, all felt too loud. He felt like putting his hands over his ears just to get it all to stop, to give him a few seconds of peace. He had no idea how he was once used to ignoring his heightened senses.

"Hey," Husher cupped his face and Jared sincerely hoped he didn't have any blood on it at the moment. "Breathe, you can get another bottle when you finish your wrap. Just listen to me."

Jared didn't quite understand why he was talking to him like he was five or something but noticed the worried looks of his friends and the sheriff. Maybe he wasn't as good at masking his facial expressions as he thought. He didn't know when his friends even came into the room.

Either way, he looked back to Husher and took a moment to focus on him. Jared's shoulders dropped once he smelt the vague scent of pine, relaxing slightly as Husher took a seat next to him.

The panic of it all was dying down as he took another bite of the chicken wrap he always ordered at the diner, which was hands down his favorite food.

He focused his ears on Husher's heart. It was steady, familiar, and grounding enough to get him through his meal before he was handed another bottle of synthetic blood.

"Joel was helping the Graham family transport drugs," Jared felt himself blurt out. "And I'm pretty sure Stephanie is connected to it too, though I can't say for sure with that one at least."

Samuel didn't look shocked, but he did look much more tired than he was before.

"Cheryl, Jordan, and Sabrina told me the same thing," he muttered. "He will be held overnight and dealt with."

"I knew it!" Mason screamed much too loud for the starting headache Jared had.

"I just have a bit of paperwork to deal with, but for the time being we can revisit this tomorrow. I have what I need from most of you," Samuel informed them.

How long was Jared out of it?

"I'll get you rooms at the bed and breakfast," Samuel informed Cheryl and the two Grahams with her. "As far as the rest of you, go home and I will call you if I need anything else."

Jared was not prepared for the attention the Carden family met him with when he walked back out into the main area and was pulled into a crushing hug by Nicole and Dawn—even Ava joined in at some point.

"Oh, honey we were so worried," Dawn murmured in his ear.

Jared let himself relax into the comforting arms.

"Sorry," Jared whispered back.

It was all he could say. How was he supposed to make up for all the worries he had caused his friends and family? He knew he didn't mean to hurt them or worry them, but the uneasy feeling was not going away no matter how much he tried to ignore it.

"Okay, you're crushing him," Husher cut in.

He wasn't totally wrong; werewolves gave hugs with everything they had. It was equal parts comforting and safe as it was mildly concerning with how much it felt like home. All the safety and security werewolves could bring, the abundance of love always baffled Jared.

"Yeah, that was the only reason," Ava chuckled.

"Definitely nothing to do with the fact *he* wanted to hug him," Mason grinned.

"I hate the both of you," Husher stated.

"I second that," Jared said with an equally blank stare. He could do without their comments for the time being.

By the time they were able to leave, Jared was tired for a different reason this time. He felt fed and warm and able to walk without seeing spots, but he felt like so much had happened in such little time.

Why not make it better—or possibly worse?

When they stepped outside Jared thought it was now or never. He pulled on the sleeve of Husher's hoodie, letting their families walk ahead of them. Jared saw his friends pause for a moment, looking back at him as if they knew what he was finally going to do. Lee gave him the thumbs up and he ignored Mason's hand gesture altogether.

When he was faced with the familiar hazel-green eyes it was not nearly as scary as he thought it would have been. Then again, for nearly three months he had been stuck living a nightmare, so most things were not nearly as scary. He needed to get this over with before it ate him alive or before he missed the chance to be truthful with his best friend.

"Hey, what's wrong—" Husher tilted his head, making him look even more like a confused puppy than he normally did.

"Shut up—I'm tired, but I refuse to leave without doing this," Jared stepped closer. He ignored his shaking hands and stood on his toes to cup the blond's face. The stupid face he couldn't just like as a friend should. "I'm going to kiss you and then run away."

He waited for a second, leaving enough room for Husher to intervene—to say no and push him away. When that didn't happen, but rather warm hands fell to his waist and pulled him closer, Jared leaned in. The simple kiss wasn't anything much, but Jared was pretty sure he would have joined the leaves on the ground if not for Husher half holding him up. Jared didn't trust his fangs not to act up again to do anything other than a quick peck on the lips before he grinned.

Cause *holy shit*—he actually just did that.

He kissed Husher Carden, and the blond kissed him back.

"I'll explain later," Jared assured him. "Just to sum it up though, that was not platonic."

"Yeah, I kinda got that when you cupped my face," Husher laughed before letting go of Jared.

He looked at Husher for a moment before sharing an equally dorky grin and flashing his fangs in a smile, then turned back in the direction of the diner.

As promised, Jared started running back to the diner before he could blurt something else out or have any time for his anxiety to lie to him. He felt like he was high off something, and whatever it was, he wanted more of it.

Chapter Twenty
They Are Both Idiots, Your Honor

Husher Garden – 29, November
(Wednesday)

It was past midnight by the time Husher had gotten home.

He could still feel the ghost of Jared's kiss on his lips, which only made him want to turn back and run to the diner to ask if that had really just happened.

He also didn't want to leave Jared out of sight after everything. He knew better, though. Things would be fine and that he would see him in a few hours when he would rush over to the diner on a totally valid breakfast run that had nothing to do with Jared... even if he knew everyone would see right through his plan.

Husher's parents were waiting for him by the door, Ava having gone inside already. His moms smiled at him and it felt like a relief to be home again.

He always did get homesick extremely easily.

When he looked at the both of them they seemed to share the same relief he did. He felt a bit sorry for scaring them by venturing off in the middle of the night without informing them and just leaving a vague note on the kitchen counter. Husher knew if he had to, though, he would do it again.

"Well, that went better than I thought it would," his mom spoke first.

Husher bent down to greet Rooty and Marco, their tails wagging, and in Rooty's case, his entire backend wigging from the speed of his tail.

"It really did," Ava agreed from the living room. "Bet Hush really liked the end of his night."

Nicole and Dawn looked confused for a moment, but Husher could tell Ava wasn't going to shut up and leave it alone. His sister started making kissy faces, and their parents seemed to understand sooner than he would have liked. He was surprised by the kiss himself—not that he didn't like it—not the point. He did not need to be teased about it only minutes afterward. Jared still had some things to tell him, and while he said the kiss was nothing platonic, Husher was still so confused that Jared freaking Baylor kissed him.

"I'm going to shower and go to bed," Husher stated, ignoring his sister.

His mama stopped him before he could leave the uncomfortable conversation he did not want to be having at the moment or ever really. Instead of asking questions, she pulled him into a hug which soon turned into a family hug. Ava joined too, picking up Marco, and Rooty jumped up out of excitement rather than out of any knowledge of what was actually going on.

"Okay, enough," Husher complained.

"What? Keep hugging you?" Ava questioned, sarcastic as ever.

Husher sighed. "Funny."

They let go of him after a minute and he was able to shower. Throwing his dirty clothes into the hamper to deal with later, he let the warm water run down his face for a moment. The smell of his pine body wash took over the whole room along with the steam of the water fogging up the mirror.

He was not only tired but rather drained.

He rinsed off and changed into clean clothes. Comfy joggers, a t-shirt with a frog living in a strawberry house on it, the matching boxer briefs because he was exactly the type of person to have a full outfit set of something with ridiculous drawings covering it.

At least it wasn't the most ridiculous thing he owned; that would be the adult pajama set Mason got him... with her face printed all over it as a gag gift that he still kept to embarrass her—it never worked though.

He grabbed his red slippers and walked back out to the living room to watch a bit of TV before bed. He didn't want to be alone at the moment.

It seemed like his family had the same idea. A movie channel was on in the background playing a film with a cheerleader trying to kill someone or something along those lines. Husher had only watched part of it. His family was all settled on the couch, Rooty and Marco lying on the fluffy rug close by.

Husher knew as soon as he sat down he would be sleeping within minutes.

Husher didn't know what time it was when he woke up. The room around him was still dark except for the light of the TV still playing in the background.

He felt wide awake at this point.

He looked over to his parents who were both still sleeping on the other end of the sectional couch. Ava sat between them, taking up the most space of anyone on the couch, and with the way she was sprawled out, she would most likely wake up with a neckache.

Quietly Husher got up, moving slowly so as to not alert either of the dogs as he made his way off the couch and walked over to the kitchen. He felt way too awake to try and fall back asleep. He just needed a bit of air and headed to the back deck, opening the door as quietly as he could and closing it behind him without alerting anyone in the house. He wrapped himself in the blanket he had grabbed from the couch and walked over to the swing in their backyard that his mom had built for his mama for their ten-year anniversary. He lay back and pushed back with the heels of his feet, rocking the swing back and forth.

The chilly air felt nice and even the vague eeriness of being outside didn't seem to bother him. He looked up at the stars, but only a handful were bright enough to notice, the dark sky relaxing him back into the swing listening to the sounds he was familiar with, sounds of the night in a place he grew up listening to.

Husher closed his eyes.

He zoned out a bit as he sat there, processing everything that had happened. It felt like only a few minutes had passed before he was brought back to reality—or rather startled when he felt the swing shift as if someone had sat down beside him. Before Husher could open his eyes he was poked in the forehead. The smell of apple pie relaxed him back into the swing when he noticed it was Jared and not someone coming out from the wooded area behind his house.

"Hi," Jared greeted him.

Husher was still in a bit of a panic from Jared just appearing. He always thought it was a vampire thing, but when he asked about it, Jared said he never noticed.

Husher opened the blanket, letting Jared take half since he was always cold.

For a moment they didn't say anything. They sat and looked at the dark sky as it lightened, the stars becoming fainter. Husher didn't know what to say—he didn't even know what to ask. He was used to being the more talkative one of their friend group—Mason sometimes taking first place for overall loudness, but none of them ever minded.

"You remember when Mas would force us to go camping with her?" Jared asked.

"And then when we heard something we would try to sneak into the house, but she always forced us to stay out there; yeah, I've never heard such colorful language from a ten-year-old," Husher answered.

Jared chuckled. "Yeah, she even threatened to glue us to our sleeping bags."

Husher winced knowing she would have actually gone through with it. In her defense, it had taken weeks of convincing their parents to sleep out in the backyard in a tent, hours to set everything up themselves, and the stories by the small campfire Mason's dad built and made sure was out before they went to bed.

"What brought that memory up?" Husher asked.

Jared kicked at the ground, pushing the swing, and Husher let him take control of it as he waited for the answer.

"I was scared then... but you were there," Jared whispered. "You were always there when I needed you or when you just wanted to hang out with me. I never understood why—still don't—but," he trailed off admittedly.

Husher never realized it.

Husher was an extrovert at heart, so he never questioned the days he spent with Jared were more than the days they spent apart. He made him happy, so, of course, he was going to be there, not just when it was convenient or easy for him to be around.

His parents raised him better than that.

Being there because he wanted to be was second nature for Husher.

"It seemed so much easier in my head," Jared muttered after a moment. "I was going to tell you that night we went on a walk that I liked you."

Husher smiled, clearly confused but happy nonetheless. "Yeah, man. I like you too. Why was that any different than the *'I love you's'* at the end of all of our conversations?"

"For fuck's sake," Jared laughed. "You're such an idiot."

He turned to face Husher and cupped his face again, the feeling of the last time he did still fresh in Husher's brain.

Oh.

"Oh," Husher gulped.

He felt his face burn as it most likely turned the same shade as his shoes. So he wasn't just imagining it?! Jared Baylor liked him. Like-liked him and not just as bros who kissed or something.

Holy shit.

Jared must have noticed how confused he was, because before Husher could tell him that he was right and the blond stereotypes might be true for him—Jared was pulling back.

"I understand if you don't want to be friends—"

Husher cut him off.

Taking his chance, he closed the distance between them and kissed the brunet. Husher pulled back, quickly forgetting he never asked Jared if he wanted to kiss him, and so he met the sweet chocolate brown eyes and nearly lost his nerve out of pure gay panic.

"I—uh—can I kiss you again?" Husher mentally face-palmed at how awkward he felt.

Jared, on the other hand, seemed to be enjoying himself, smiling up at him with a grin to rival the full moon. The jittery energy was the same, and he was too stunned to turn away from such a smile being focused on him.

"I would kick you if you didn't," Jared informed him, rubbing his thumb along Husher's cheek.

Husher still looked confused. "So you *like* me?"

"Have for a while, thought I'd try a more direct approach with it."

"I just assumed you didn't like anyone. You're telling me the crush I had since elementary school likes me back?!" Husher exclaimed.

Jared looked at him wide-eyed. "Elementary school?"

"I'd always draw us together and talk about how we would get a house and probably a cat named something ridiculously adorable like Madam Meows or something when we grow up."

It seemed like it was Jared's turn to look confused.

"I just thought it was because you were a werewolf and they were more affectionate towards their friends," Jared admitted.

Husher thought about it for a moment; he did have a point. He wasn't confirmed as a beta until he was sixteen. Betas were much more laidback about most things, less affected by the scents of others, and didn't have to deal with all the things alphas and omegas did. From an outsider's perspective, though, he would have never known the difference between werewolf-level friendships and any other living beings.

"Why didn't you tell me sooner?!" Husher put his hand over his mouth after shouting across the backyard.

"To be fair, I also thought I didn't like anyone," Jared shrugged. "Clued in I was demisexual around the same time I realized wanting to kill your best friend's boyfriend was not a 'normal' thing."

Husher leaned down enough to rest his head on Jared's shoulder.

"So we are both idiots?" Husher asked.

"Seems like it, yeah."

It might have taken a moment for Husher to process it all, but when he did it didn't seem to be all that shocking when he looked back on the years of apparently mutual pining.

"Just to be clear, we are boyfriends now or—" Husher trailed off, not really sure how to ask other than that.

"Well, Hush, do you want to be my boyfriend?" Jared asked with a soft smile.

Husher didn't even hesitate. "Very much."

Jared didn't seem all that fazed and instead wrapped more of the blanket over himself before sighing. "Okay I accept, but I am very demanding."

"Oh really?" Husher asked, knowing he truthfully wasn't—and even if Jared was, he would be willing to do anything the vampire told him to.

"Yep," Jared nodded, popping the 'p' at the end.

"Like what?" Husher questioned.

"I demand good morning texts," Jared said matter-of-factly.

"I do that already."

Husher had done that ever since he could remember. What started as wake-up calls for school turned into a morning routine most of the time. Even when Jared would only fall back to sleep by the end of the call he still kept calling and talking about nothing as he got ready.

"I know."

"What else?" Husher asked.

Jared thought for a moment before resting his head on Husher's shoulder. The contact wasn't anything new. Being friends as long as they had been, Jared was used to Husher's love language being a mix of physical touch and acts of service. And Husher was used to Jared's being sarcastic comments and cooking.

"Couple costumes next year for Halloween," Jared finally spoke.

"I think I can manage that."

Jared laced their hands together and Husher finally felt his nerves fall away.

He didn't even know he fell asleep until he was hit in the shoulder with a tennis ball and nearly fell off the swing—taking Jared down with him.

"Found him!" Ava yelled from the back deck.

Husher felt Jared's hand still holding his, balancing the both of them back on the swing. Husher didn't question it as he put his head back on Jared's shoulder. It was a problem for later; right now, he just needed five more minutes.

Chapter Twenty-One
The One Man Musical

Jared Baylor – 01, December (Friday)

Waking up in his own bed was something Jared was slowly getting used to. The warm sunlight that crept into his room along the green leaves of the plants that had taken over his bedroom. Jared was not a morning person most of the time, but he seemed to appreciate them much more as he got up and ready for a morning shift at the diner. He checked his phone, falling back asleep when Husher had called him earlier.

Things had gone back to somewhat normal, for the most part. Living above the diner with Moon again and being told to drink whatever tea she handed him. Stirring the blend with the intentions he wanted to set for the day, he didn't question her magic and sipped the hot tea while he rushed around the apartment grabbing just the right shade of black clothing in his mess of a closet then sitting on the couch as he tied his new red shoes that he needed to add some pins to or something. The demi pin he had was still on the stuffed animal Sabrina had with her, so he would have to see if Mason could make him some more. He finished the tea and made sure to wash the *'world's best plant dad'* mug out, since it was the one he usually drank out of. He grabbed his phone and headed downstairs to hear the newest town gossip and get his second dose of tea for the day.

News of Joel and Stephanie working with the Graham family selling and transporting drugs traveled fast. The town was divided in shock and unamused suspicion. Jared genuinely wished he saw the moment Joel noticed he was fucked and that his badge wasn't going to help him get out of the things he had done, even though the town paper did a pretty good job at showing the shocked look on his face when he was taken out in cuffs. It was one of the few times Jared read the newspaper. Skipping over the segment about him no longer being missing when he read: *"local vampire gets lost and abducted all the while having no idea what was actually happening"* he moved to the image of Joel trying not to notice the camera.

Going back to work at the diner was surprisingly a lot easier than he thought it would be. Years of memorizing his tasks hadn't faded away while he tried to regain his health. Rushing out of the kitchen with too many plates of food was oddly comforting when it all came back to him like muscle memory.

The diner was full of familiar faces and the smell of freshly baked sweets being placed behind the glass that morning. Jared never expected to miss the morning rush quite as much as he thought. He could do without the people asking if he was okay, but the news was still fresh and he knew it was bound to happen when living in such a small town.

Jared looked up at the door when it chimed open revealing a cleaner and happy version of Cheryl and Sabrina. Cheryl's hair was down and out of her usual braids, so it took Jared a moment to notice it was her. Sabrina too seemed to change, her long and mostly matted hair was cut to her shoulders and one simple braid was mixed into the back like the knot magic Moon had in some of her witchy books about; a symbol that guards the person from negative frequencies, protecting the person's positive energy.

"Jared!" Sabrina screamed.

Jared tried not to cover his ears. He was pretty sure the kid could rival Mason in a banshee-screaming match. He half hoped there was another 'Jared' there that he had failed to notice, but it was too late; he made eye contact and figuratively walked himself into a corner.

"Hey, to you too."

"I thought the festival would be fun for her to see," Cheryl explained.

Jared nodded. He knew that when they got out that Cheryl was working on adopting Sabrina, but he wasn't sure what had come of the whole process. When Moon legally adopted him, the process took longer than he wanted. It would be a while before things were able to become *'normal'* for them again. With the trauma Cheryl and Sabrina had been through, there were a lot of pros to keeping them together.

Then there was Jordan.

Jared had no idea what would happen to him. After Jared got back to town he knew Jordan confessed to the fire, but it wasn't like he was the most mentally fit person.

Jared was too happy to be out of the house and away from the Grahams he didn't care about much else.

"The winter festival is the best time to visit!" Jared exclaimed. "Unless you hate the cold. Then I don't suggest it, I guess." The winter festival was always one of the times he appreciated living in a small town. The cozy charm of traditions passed down, people visiting, and the time spent with friends and family doing something they only got to do at certain times a year.

"It really is a cute town," Cheryl said in a bit of awe as she sat down at the counter.

Sabrina was already spinning in the bar stool, clearly in awe of the place too. Then again, she didn't know much about the outside world. Everything was new and wonderful.

"What's a good drink for this winter festival?" Cheryl asked.

Working at the diner for years Jared was fully prepared if people asked what the specials were, what he would order, or what was good—which was always weird to answer since he had no idea what *they* considered good. Though working again and having unlimited fruit punch to drink in front of the customers and freaking a few of them out was a highlight to dealing with the few annoying or rude ones.

Jared grabbed some menus and handed them over, both being coloring sets because Moon refused to give out boring menus just because someone was an adult. Plus, it was great for business, even with the amount of crayons they went through.

"Hot chocolate is a must," Jared informed her. "But we also have seasonal coffees."

"Banana hot chocolate," Sabrina demanded without missing a beat.

The diner had several flavors for their hot chocolate, some of which horrified and disgusted Jared. He didn't know whether to be mortified or disgusted that something like raspberry hot chocolate could exist or even the white hot chocolate, but they were both surprisingly good.

Jared nodded, not wanting to get on the bad side of the child, and he gave Cheryl another minute. By the time he came back with Sabrina's order, Cheryl was ready to order a classic hot chocolate, which took no time to make and added the whipped cream with chocolate shavings on the top.

"Wow," Sabrina said. Whipped cream on her face from her own drink, Cheryl chuckled and handed over a napkin before thanking Jared.

"Yeah, no worries. Hope you enjoy your time here," Jared said before walking over to clear the next table and letting them enjoy their drinks.

It wouldn't be long until his shift was up and Husher would be coming to get him so they could enjoy the festival. Lee and Mason promised to meet them at some point like they always did. Outside the diner, people had mostly set up all their booths, games, and activities that were planned. The theme must have had something to do with gnomes since Jared kept seeing them everywhere outside—or a new nightmare would be coming true and they would be taking over the town. He seriously needed to stay away from the movies his friends recommended him to watch.

It wouldn't be until later that the town would be lit up with twinkly lights, the stores' and shops' with bright display windows would be the most beautiful they'd be all year. It was like being in a movie, especially with all the people staying or visiting for the season and taking pictures.

By the time Husher showed up Jared was finishing up his shift as promised. It was the perfect time to leave for the lunch rush. Quickly Jared finished up with his last table and clocked out before rushing to Moon's office—today it was the kitchen, tomorrow who knew.

"Leaving, I'll be back later," Jared said, out of breath from rushing around and trying to get words out at the same time.

"Okay, okay, breathe." Moon rolled her eyes. "Enjoy your date."

He was halfway out of the kitchen before processing what she had said.

"It's not a—never mind."

There was no point arguing with her.

In his rush he nearly tripped over nothing on his way back out front. He looked around to see if anyone noticed and groaned when his eyes met Husher's.

"How long have you been standing there?"

"Long enough to see the invisible goblin trip you."

Jared flicked his arm. "Oh, shut the fuck up, I'll have one trip you."

Husher wasn't bothered by his comment and shrugged it off knowing he wasn't as prone to tripping over absolutely nothing like Jared was.

"Ready?" Husher asked.

Jared nodded, replacing his apron with his hoodie before dragging the blond out the door. It was much louder outside, music playing from one of the booths.

He was welcomed with the nostalgic scent of kettle corn as he walked closer to the food area of the town event.

"They really do go all out," Jared said, almost not believing it despite the years he lived there.

"You should see the cookies," Husher informed him. "Ava got one decorated like her face."

Husher pulled out his phone and showed Jared the picture of Ava with a sugar cookie version of her face, then he swiped to show Ava taking a bite of the cookie, leaving the sugar cookie version of her face with one less eye.

"That is terrifying, and we are totally doing that," Jared informed him.

Husher didn't argue. Instead, they walked around the stalls and tables set up until they found the cookie one.

"Hi, two cookies of our faces—never thought I'd say that!" Husher exclaimed.

The woman behind the table only chuckled before getting two face-shaped sugar cookies and piping the icing with the cookie-free hand. Jared was pretty sure he didn't blink as he watched her add the different layers and completely freehand the design. When she packaged them up, Jared was still impressed. Husher paid her and Jared was handed the cookies until they could find a good place to sit and eat them.

"I don't think I will be able to icing a sugar cookie ever again without being ashamed," Jared informed his now-boyfriend.

"How will you go on?"

"Don't know, it might actually be the end of me."

Husher rolled his eyes.

It didn't take them long to find Lee and their cousins. The one the same height as Lee was Cody. He was only a year younger than Lee but dressed like an old man, wearing a sweater vest and a hat that covered black as coal hair.

Trinity Cleamon was the blonde and one of the taller ten-year-olds Jared had the unfortunate pleasure of meeting.

"Hey guys," Lee muttered.

They were playing a basketball game and Lee was winning if the frowns on the other two Cleamon's faces were anything to go from.

"Hey," Husher greeted. "You know that you being the oldest doesn't mean you have to win all the games, right?"

"I am not winning all of the games," Lee said in their defense.

"You have won nine so far," Cody deadpanned.

Jared knew better than to think Lee would go easy on someone when it came to games or any competition. They would fight to win. Jared had yet to win any board game with them and it had been years of defeat.

"I am not that bad," Lee murmured. They threw the ball, which swooshed in the basket, bringing the total wins to ten. There were only a few more games left that they hadn't played, and Jared knew just as well as anyone else that they would win those too.

"Yeah, definitely," Cody said sarcastically.

Lee waved them off. "Whatever, go find your dad before he gets into another fight with Debra and Grandma has to break it up. I am not dealing with another food color incident."

The Cleamon family was nice for the most part. Jared liked how going over there was like walking into a crystal shop thanks to Lee's grandma. However, Debra and Brett were like some kind of nightmare twins. Even at the age of thirty-nine, they bickered about the most random things. As far as Lee's mom, she was cut off when Lee was born, leaving them behind with their grandmother.

"Fine, but don't forget the cotton candy you promised us," Trinity informed her cousin.

Lee nodded and put their new keychain they won into their fanny pack that if it wasn't ugly enough—the neon yellow color did the job. It looked way too much like the shade of a highlighter or the shorts Husher wore in middle school.

"Are you going to go through all the games again this year or are you going to join us and watch this year's play?" Husher asked.

Jared and Lee both groaned at the thought of having to sit through another play. Written, directed, and acted by one person, picked at random each year. They were always so bad and, of course, Husher fucking loved them despite his protest to most well-acted, directed, and written plays, and musicals.

"Remind me who won this year?" Lee asked, looking as amused as Jared was about it.

"Ronnie," Husher answered. "You literally work with him at the grocery store."

"I tolerate my coworkers," Lee reminded him. "And all he does is talk about his ex-girlfriend who was *the sweetest person he had ever met*. It's nauseating, and I feel bad for his ex for just knowing him let alone dating him."

"They have a point," Jared nodded.

"What? No, we are going. You both agreed to it and I have the texts to prove it," Husher piped in.

"Then why ask?" Lee deadpanned.

"To be nice," Husher informed them.

Jared vaguely remembered the conversation, but it didn't mean he was happy about having to watch a one-man show starring someone he didn't even consider a man or person in general.

However, much like Lee, he reluctantly walked to the outdoor theater.

"I'm sure it won't be that bad," Husher insisted.

Jared grabbed the cookie of Husher's face and without missing a beat he looked him dead in the eyes as he bit into it, tearing off the side of his sugar cookie face.

"Rude," Husher commented and took the cookie of Jared's face.

"You know, when I think *I'm* being dramatic I'll remember this moment," Lee said, watching them.

Jared flipped them off and quickly sat down before the play started. For a moment Jared thought maybe—just maybe—his boyfriend was right and that the play would not be as bad as last year or even the year before that.

Nope; it was exactly that bad.

Jared didn't know how it could have been that awful. The mean comments he made in his head were enough to entertain himself through the performance and were some of his best work. The only thing that would have made the play fun was if he was allowed to verbally scream out what was floating around in his head.

"Okay, so I didn't think it would be a musical of his life." Husher put his hands up in defense once the play was over.

"I am pretty sure he didn't think it was going to be a musical until five minutes before the show," Jared guessed.

When the play was over they walked over to some of the tables to see what people were selling or giving out.

Conveniently, it didn't take long for Mason to find them *after* the show. She walked over to them and slung her arm over him and Husher, cutting into the middle.

"Where were you?" Husher asked.

"Avoiding the shit show."

"Fair enough," Jared shrugged.

Mason nodded. "Exactly."

Husher seemed to leave it alone after that, knowing better than to argue when the play wasn't really worth it.

"Game time?" Lee asked.

They nodded and Jared followed them over to the section of the town square that had the games setup. There were a few crowds, and the lines of people waiting for the booths weren't too bad. The games they had were fairly simple. Ring tossing, balloon popping, and basic carnival games were the most popular. It was easy to fall back into normalcy and play the games thoughtlessly. Lee took most of the prizes and Mason won a mushroom plushie she was happy about.

Jared let Husher pull him along to the games.

When they were done they went and got some food, mostly town favorites or winter classics.

Lee was on their phone and turned it back with a smile.

"It's going to snow tonight," Lee informed them.

Before they could do anything else Husher handed back the container of popcorn they got. Jared felt the flash of light better than he saw it. When he looked up at Mason she only winked at him.

"What the hell was that?" Jared asked, blinking the flash of her camera away.

"Oh, nothing."

Husher, unfortunately, did not take the flash so well because he ended up backing up and bumping into someone. That someone happened to be Tiffany Shaffer, the mayor's wife and the person Husher had accidentally hit with a pie twice.

Mason doubled over laughing, Husher turned slowly before slipping behind Jared, and Lee waved.

"Sorry," Husher blurted.

"It's fine." Tiffany was unharmed and laughed it off before walking to one of the booths.

"Dude," Mason began but started laughing again before she could finish what she was saying.

"You good?" Jared asked.

Husher shook his head, but two seconds later nodded.

Jared let it go and they walked back to the diner for hot chocolate and to warm up a little before checking out a few more places and calling it a night. They all sat in a booth, him and Husher on one side and Lee and Mason on the other. It was kinda funny how drinking hot chocolate, something so simple, felt as comforting as it did when he was with his friends. The day and start of the night didn't make up for lost time and it would take a while before things were okay again, but for right now, this seemed like enough.

Husher rested his head on Jared's shoulder, sleepy from the long day. Jared, without thought, kissed him on the head and felt another flash that seemed to stay on them. Jared knew it had to be a video at this point.

He flipped Mason off.

Husher moved back and took a sip of his hot chocolate, blocking the light with his hand.

"Wow, I am going to love sharing an apartment with you," Mason replied, unbothered. "At least some of the sexual tension is gone."

Husher spit out his hot chocolate, most of it going back into his cup.

"That was rude," Lee deadpanned.

All Jared could do was laugh at the look on his boyfriend's face.

Chapter Twenty-Two
Everyone Just Shut Up

Husher Carden – 03, December (Sunday)

Husher woke up on the floor, which was pretty disorienting since he remembered being on the couch with Jared when he fell asleep. Jared, Mason, and Lee had all invited themselves over for a movie night. It was something they would always do whenever they had the time, and since it was December, there wasn't much they wanted to do outside unless it was one of the random warm days or a snow day. Those were always taken seriously.

Husher groaned a bit from sleeping on the floor for most of the night. He still had no idea how he got there. He looked over to where he should have been lying and saw Jared face down on the couch, one arm holding a stuffed star plushie Lee won from the festival. His other arm was dangling over the edge of the couch and almost hitting Husher in the face.

That explained it.

Jared might have been the smallest in the group, but he somehow took up the most space. Husher was reminded of the movie night he had to share the couch with Jared and Ava—in the end, he had grabbed a few pillows and sat on the floor. It was much better than having a foot to his rib cage or face.

Husher sat up looking around the living room, ignoring the ache in his limbs, and quietly stood.

Mason was on the other end of the couch taking up most of the space, her head nearly hanging over the edge, and the blankets kicked off completely. Husher was pretty sure she was a close second to Jared and Ava for the personal space thing as well. Lee had brought their own roll-up mattress, wanting to get a good night of sleep and also taking up a normal amount of room as they had pillows and blankets wrapped around them.

It was too early to get up, but Husher knew if he went back to sleep it would only end with him being even more tired. So, he walked back to his room in the dim early morning light. Quietly, he picked out a clean pair of clothes before walking to the bathroom and turning on the light. He cringed at the brightness before he blinked his vision back and turned on the shower to warm up. He threw his old clothes into the hamper and got into the steaming shower, taking an extra minute for hot water to melt his back in hopes of getting rid of the aches and pain of sleeping on the floor.

Going about his normal morning routine and taking the time to actually moisturize the added consequences of the cold weather drying his skin out. By the time he walked back out to the living room his teeth were brushed, he was showered, and dressed in clean clothes.

He walked back the hallway to see if his parents were up before he acted as the alarm and was louder than a DJ from New Jersey waking up his friends.

He knocked on the open door. Usually, they were all morning people, but he still didn't want to be rude to his parents. His mama looked up from her book, still in bed reading, while his mom was styling her hair at her vanity. Dawn sat her book down when she was finished with the page before turning her attention to her son. "Buenos días, corazón."

Husher made himself at home in his parents' room. He walked in and sat at the foot of the bed before falling back dramatically into the fluffy, cloud-like bedding.

"Morning, Mama," Husher murmured. "I was going to wake them up and didn't want to wake you guys in the process."

"Don't use my new pots for it this time," his mom demanded.

Husher looked over and put his hands up when she pointed the curling iron at him jokingly. He nodded, knowing better than to actually mess anything up in the kitchen, whether he was cooking or just getting supplies to wake up his friends.

"I would never," Husher murmured into the comforter.

"Sure you wouldn't. Get Ava up too while you're playing the life of an alarm clock this morning," his mom replied.

With that, Husher slid off their bed and walked out to the kitchen to grab the supplies he would need: an old pot from the cabinet and a wooden spoon from the drawer near the stove. The year he had played drums when he was nine came in handy in moments like these.

He took a deep breath and without hesitation walked closer to the open living room and hit the old pot as loud as he could while screaming, "Wake up!" to his loving friends. Lee sat straight up, which always freaked Husher out when they did that. There was no way someone could sleep so stiffly and be okay. Jared was next but not as graceful as the elf. He rolled off the couch and onto the floor, the fluffy rug helping soften the fall, but there was still a soft thud.

Mason was last and didn't react much other than sleepily opening her eyes and then closing them and going back to sleep.

"Hush, shut the fuck up!" Jared screamed.

Husher only walked back to the other hallway and past his room to Ava's. He stood out of the door for a little, hitting the pot and screaming for her to wake up. He waited for her to get up and open the door yelling at him or something along the lines of what Jared did.

Once everyone was awake Husher waited for his friends to get ready—putting the pot and wooden spoon back in the kitchen—before they all walked to the diner for breakfast.

"My ear is still ringing," Jared complained.

"Maybe you should answer it," Husher suggested.

He stopped walking, sighing deeply, and turned to face Husher as if he were questioning everything all at once and was not getting paid enough to exist.

"Why am I willingly dating you?" Jared deadpanned.

"Because my charm is *so* good, your demisexual self went *'yep, that one,'* and you have not known peace since you fell hopelessly in love with me."

Jared blinked before sighing again. "You're not wrong."

Mason fake gagged at them. "Guys, not before my hot chocolate intake for the morning."

"I'm siding with Mas on this one. You two go be a lovey dovey couple somewhere else."

"Oh, so I have to listen to all the things you wanna do to the new receptionist at the garage, at *two* in the morning—which mind you, the list of things you *wouldn't* do to her was shorter," Husher looked at Mason, "but I can't say something completely PG to my boyfriend?"

"Yes, exactly," Mason nodded. "Don't know why we call you the himbo of the group when you're that smart."

"Both of you shut up," Jared interrupted.

He grabbed Husher's hand—shutting him up quickly—and pulled him along the rest of the way to the diner.

It always smelled like paradise in the diner all the cozy comforting vibes packed into one place. Baked goods, ground coffee, and whatever specials they had for the day all mixed so well together. Husher never truthfully got used to it but having a diner walking distance from his house was one of the perks of living in Lones Lake.

Husher followed after Jared and over to one of the tables near the window. Since it was the west side of the diner the sunlight wouldn't be an issue. People watching on a laid-back Sunday was half the fun, after all.

Jared let go of Husher's hand when he took his seat by the window. Husher sat on the opposite side of him so he could have a window seat as well. Lee sat beside Jared and Mason beside Husher, who pushed him closer to the window when she sat down even though there was plenty of room between them.

"Stop acting like toddlers," Lee whispered.

Which Husher knew was a losing game, and he was just grateful it was Moon's diner and the likelihood of getting kicked out was pretty low. Not impossible, but low enough Husher was unbothered to act any different. Jared just watched the two adults who did in fact act like toddlers more times than not.

"He is too fucking close," Mason snapped.

"I am way over here." Husher pointed his finger at her but didn't touch her, which always pissed Mason off.

"You're an ass is what you are," Mason corrected.

Husher clutched his non-existent pearls. "Rude."

Mason smiled. "Thank you."

They were interrupted by the waitress. "What can I get y'all?" Eve asked.

Mason pushed Husher back by the face and ordered her usual blueberry waffles and a blueberry hot chocolate to match.

"Switching it up from the classic today," Eve stated as she wrote down the order.

Mason nodded before removing her hand from Husher's face so he could order. The promise of food usually calmed them down.

"I'll have strawberry buttermilk pancakes with a mug of strawberry milk," Husher ordered.

"Do you think they realize how too much of one thing is never good?" Lee asked Jared.

Jared shook his head, knowing better. Husher knew not everyone liked sweets at all or in the mornings. Husher was not one of those people and liked to order anything strawberry. Lee joined in shaking their head as well, not understanding how anyone could eat so many sweets with fruit-flavored meals paired with the same flavored drink.

"Okie dokie, and for you?" Eve asked. Lee ordered the biggest glass of pulp-filled orange juice they could, two scrambled eggs and a raspberry sticky bun that was on the special that day. Then it was Jared's time to order. He stuck with a classic—at least for him—fluffy scrambled eggs, home fries with peppers, and a mug of fruit punch.

Eve nodded and went back to send their orders to the kitchen. The diner was comfortably busy, but it was still early enough not to wait too long for their food. Eve brought out their drinks in record time before moving to the next table.

"How are you going to live with both of them?" Lee asked.

Husher looked up mid-shove from Mason, who seemed to pause for Jared's answer too. Sure, Husher knew they were a bit much to deal with for some people, and moving in with friends could go horribly wrong, but knowing what he did about his friends, he didn't think there would be any major problems. Would they bicker more than Ava and he did? Absolutely. Would they flip each other off at random? It was as promised as the sun rising. But he didn't think there was anything major that they wouldn't get over within a day or two. Husher was too excited about them getting an apartment together to be nervous about it. January was only a little while away, and he was just glad to have finally found a place big enough for the three of them. They had asked Lee to move in as well, but they declined for the time being. They still had a few classes to finish for high school, and despite having a plan for everything, Lee had no idea what they wanted to attend college for since they were able to do what they wanted now and work as a cashier on the side.

"They both react to food," Jared finally answered Lee.

Husher went to argue then closed his mouth, and Mason did the same, both realizing why Jared always handed one of them a snack when they were arguing.

"Exactly." Jared nodded. "They are easy enough to deal with."

Husher let the conversation end when he got his food. He was hungry; it wasn't like he was proving Jared right about anything as he stopped bothering Mason to eat his perfectly crispy on the outside and fluffy on the inside pancakes.

"So what are we doing about the furniture?" Husher questioned after half his plate was cleared.

He wasn't sure where they were going to get stuff cheap enough since the three months' rent and the deposit weren't a walk in the park to afford. It left them with having to know a person who knows a person who is getting rid of their dead relative's things or something. They planned on taking some things from their current rooms at home but wanted to keep the basics there in case they ever stayed over for holidays or in general.

"Don't worry about it," Mason muttered. "I know someone."

Jared gave her a questioning look and Husher thought she was reading his mind or something. He didn't think she could do that—which a moment later when he thought about keying one of the old cars she was working on to get a reaction nothing came of it—so it was a safe bet she couldn't.

"It is fully legit," Mason answered his and Jared's silent question.

"Like the time we got backstage passes to that concert?" Husher asked, remembering the concert all too well and being asked to leave before security made them.

"I didn't see the typo," Mason informed him. "And it's not like that anyway. I got everything from an old storage unit they sold for a hundred bucks. All we have to do is pick it up—a couch, a kitchen table, chairs, and two-bed frames."

"And you're just now telling us?" Jared asked.

"Yeah," Mason nodded as if it were nothing. "We'll still need stuff, but it's a lot of the bigger items, so that will work for the time being at least. You two can figure out the rest since I found the place to begin with."

Husher nodded. It wouldn't be all that difficult anyway. Plus, unless he wanted different shades of a green to be their themed apartment he knew better than to leave decorating the common areas to Mason.

"Which reminds me, I need a place to put my plants," Jared informed them. As if it just now occurred to him to say something about it.

Husher looked to Mason, who only took another bite of her blueberry waffle.

"All of them?" Husher asked, slightly scared to hear the answer.

Jared stared at him blankly. "You dare ask a plant dad to choose between his children?"

"I would never do such a thing, I was just wondering how much to plan for," Husher confirmed. He had no idea how his boyfriend kept all the plants he had alive and well. His room looked more like a greenhouse each time he saw it.

"I would," Mason said. "Where the hell are we putting all of them?!"

"With the stick," Jared said with a blank face.

Husher paused.

He wouldn't.

Husher looked up at Jared and then at Lee who knew just as well as Husher did that Jared would absolutely say it.

Mason looked confused. "What stick?!"

"The one up your ass," Jared laughed.

Mason gasped in realization. "You little—"

Husher took the fork from Mason as Lee helped shield Jared.

Yeah, living together was totally going to be a breeze.

Chapter Twenty-Three
Late Night

Jared Baylor – 14, December (Thursday)

I t was late.

It would be one of the nights Jared relied on synthetic blood to keep him awake long into the daylight hours and most likely for the next twenty-four hours; otherwise, his sleep schedule would be fucked again. Really, he just needed to stay awake long enough to finish the tasks at hand. Working in a diner that doubled as a bakery was not for the weak-willed. Working for Moon in general was not for the weak, it was dedicated to the people who failed to understand what sleep was.

He was helping Moon with the food prep for an event they were supplying a few things for along with getting their normal meal preparations done for the week. Jared had lost count of the amount of bread he had to prepare and let rise before putting them into the oven for the last few hours, rushing to make other loaves to freeze. Miss Moon's Diner always had fresh baked goods on top of their normal restaurant meals, but it took constant up-keep, hours spent late at night making sure things were ready for the next day and week. It was something only someone who liked the career could put up with after so many years.

Jared hummed along to the music that was playing in the background stuck on the radio station of festive songs Moon only allowed in any month other than December because she could. She was not going to be like the rest of the town to sing carols in half the month of December. This year, she must have felt the cheer everyone in town always did, Jared had no idea what else it could have been. She even put a string of multi-colored lights up outside the diner's door. It helped brighten people's moods, and while Jared had mixed feelings about winter, it was always nice seeing twinkling lights when he looked out his windows at night. It felt nice to see Moon was still herself despite the few changes she made; she told Kristen, the mayor, where she could put the tree—Jared was pretty sure Moon was the only one who could talk to the mayor like that and get away with it.

Jared shrugged it off and walked over to grab the large bag of flour he needed before walking back over to his freshly cleaned and cleared-off workstation. He was sent to make a batch of raspberry sticky buns for pickup in the morning, which was only in a few hours, and the recipe took at least three hours from start to finish. He at least didn't have to make their normal batch which consisted of at least three people helping to prepare and freeze a few batches as well for sale at the grocery store.

"Keep the raspberry juice for the tea later," Moon told him.

The raspberries and sometimes blueberries were frozen from their summer collection. Any remaining juice, when they were unfroze, was drained and used for their special sweet tea and Jared didn't think anything else tasted as much like summer.

"I wasn't missing for that long," Jared chuckled.

Which no, he probably shouldn't have been joking so soon about it. The nightmares were still there, and he was pretty sure he would never be able to look at canned fruit ever again without wanting to die a little inside. However, humor helped him cope, and so he didn't really care how uncomfortable it made some people. Plus, he loved that tea just as much as anyone else, and he would never dare forget to save the juice from the raspberries.

"Long enough," Moon muttered with a frown, her shoulders slumped as she continued. "I was worried so bad that day Husher walked in without you."

Jared added the yeast and sugar to the warm water and milk mixture before he looked up at her. It wasn't like he didn't know he had worried a lot of people. Hell, he worried himself. It was one of the things he was working on—not feeling the guilt for since it wasn't his fault for being taken by supernatural-hating assholes. He knew it wasn't really his fault, he hadn't wanted to worry them on purpose, but he still felt fucking awful about it. Awful that he failed and felt guilty anyway.

"Don't you say it," Moon reminded him.

"I can't help it," Jared muttered.

"You can. And you will, I don't want *sorry* from you," Moon said as if it were already a fact. "You have overcome a lot of shit in your life. You will get over this too. I am proud of you, you know that right?"

Jared did in fact know that. He also knew if the woman kept talking like that he would be adding tears to the sticky buns and didn't think it would be all that sanitary.

"Yeah, you still put gold stars on my apron," Jared informed her, ignoring the lump in his throat as he turned back to his work.

She laughed. "You're never too old for stickers."

"Damn right," Jared agreed.

He grabbed another bowl and mixed the flour and salt together before grabbing the butter from the microwave. Working in the diner for as long as he has, Jared had the recipe memorized for years now. With bigger portions he did have to look at the recipe card, though; math was very much not a strong suit of his.

Jared switched on the mixer to save time kneading the dough. If it weren't for the long night he would have done it by hand like he normally liked to. When the dough was done and the sides of the mixing bowl were clean he let the dough rest in an oiled bowl before coming back to it in an hour to roll it out and to add the filling. Using dental floss was the easiest and quickest way to cut the rolls for him without the filling spilling out, wrapping the string of floss around the roll and twisting it only to pull the ends and cut the rolls perfectly.

It was all muscle memory at that point.

Energy levels depleted, he grabbed a bottle of synthetic blood. Drinking blood felt close to how energy drinks felt for humans, at least that was how it seemed when he asked his friends. Husher not being included since his ADHD made caffeine have more of a sleepy effect on him. Blood gave Jared the same level of energy as a neurotypical drinking a mango flavored energy drink, though it did give him the nutritional values his body needed unlike said energy drinks.

Being only half vampire, he was used to mixing up his diet. Human food was filling, but it left him sluggish if it was all he consumed. If he only drank blood, it didn't work out all that well with his anxiety levels, leaving him a jittery mess more times than not. So he had to do a mix of both, balancing something out to appeal to the vampire side of him and the human—which was always weird to think about given the fangs he had.

Working in the kitchen and sipping at the bottle of blood, he wondered what his ancestors would think of him. It was an oddly prideful moment imagining how disappointed they would be in him. Working in a diner with his witch guardian, having a werewolf as a boyfriend, never drinking blood from the vein, and being able to be a vampire without being killed on the grounds of being a supernatural person.

By the time the raspberry sticky buns were cooling Jared was helping clean the kitchen with Moon before he put the simple icing on top. He wrapped them up and added their ingredient sticker to the bottom of the container along with a sticker on top telling the customer it wasn't open since they were put into the container, and lastly, the diner's logo: a coffee mug with a moon in the center of it.

"Movie?" Moon asked.

Jared nodded as he washed up and moved on to help with the rest of the orders.

He would be up for hours which was what he was planning. Otherwise, he would be left crashing and sleeping most of his day away and being stuck awake all night in a cycle that he was trying hard to correct.

Moon handed the remote over to him. The TV in the kitchen seemed ridiculous to most, but on late nights it was comforting to put on a movie and bake until the sun came up, and it was a nice change from the music in the kitchen.

Nights like this were one of the reasons Jared wanted to stay closer to home. He loved his job. He liked being in town—even when the gossip made him question it. Being in the first place he could genuinely call home was not something he was going to take lightly or get rid of. He looked around the kitchen he knew like the back of his own hand. It was one of his favorite places in town. It felt like he could press pause on the rest of the world as he baked.

They made pies, something he would no doubt get comments about since Husher insisted he smelled like an apple pie most of the time. Jared didn't understand if it was a wolf thing or if he was just used to his own scent, but he didn't ever think he smelled like apple pie, the diner did. So maybe it was that. Jared helped decorate the cakes they had on order and the few that were going on display in the morning behind the glass. The cakes always went pretty quickly and frosting them was pretty fun too. He made a purple heart cake earlier and had the crumb coat chilling. He put on the final layer of buttercream, lavender, before making a few different shades of purple to pipe on the details that made it look even better. He even added edible glitter to it just to be extra.

His phone had buzzed at some point, but he didn't check it until his break since he didn't want to take his gloves off again. It was annoying having to take them off mid-task.

When he was on break, he saw that it was Lee, who had sent him a picture of Lee's uncle mid-fall from a ladder while trying to hang lights outside.

LeEeee – 04:03

image sent ✓

it's a JAr – 4:36

why is your uncle putting lights up at FOUR IN THE MORNING?!

LeEeee – 04:37

Before Debra can tell him she didn't want the clear ones up again this year. Plus he's kinda stupid.

Jared knew Debra would be taking the lights down and putting the ones she wanted up anyway, but the picture was pretty funny. It would probably make its way onto the Cleamon's holiday cards the twins' mom was in charge of putting together. It usually ended in arguments, but Jared always looked forward to seeing it each year with how funny it was.

LeEeee – 04:39

ALSO if you have any cookies—the jam ones, I need my fix.

it's a JAr – 04:40

sure, I'll put a dozen back for you

LeEeee – 04:40

Thanks, dude. You're the best

It was around then that Jared was done baking for the day—night—and the time Moon went up to bed while Jared stayed in the diner to open and start the morning rush. He would be good to go in the sleep department, so it didn't matter much to him. He made sure to put a box of cookies aside for Lee to pick up later before he forgot and went back up to the apartment to quickly shower.

Jared rushed around the apartment as quickly and silently as he could manage as he changed out of his flour-covered clothes to a pair of clean ones before he went back downstairs and put on his normal apron and switched the open sign on to get ready for his morning shift.

Chapter Twenty-Four
Worms on the Ceiling

Husher knew he was being ridiculous.

He knew that he would only be moving to the edge of town and everything was still within walking distance; it just might take a little longer to get to town by foot. Maybe he could get into jogging or something. Moving still seemed like a much more difficult task than he had originally expected it to be. It felt like he was moving miles and miles away even though he could probably see the diner from the new apartment if he squinted.

"Stop looking like you're going to hurl," Mason commented.

"I do not look like I'm going to hurl," Husher retorted. At least he didn't think he looked like that if anything he was doing better since they left his house.

"You kinda do, Hush," Jared agreed.

"I don't need this." Husher looked over to his boyfriend.

Mason slung her arm around him and pulled Jared in on her other side, which went as well as Husher would have thought.

"We are just saying, dude, lighten up a little. We have the best location for everything," Mason exclaimed.

She was right; he knew that she was. The apartment would work great for their up coming school schedule, and Mason and Jared could walk to work—if the weather was nice enough. Husher did his best to ignore the anxiety of going out of his comfort zone.

He took a breath and followed along into the building to get the keys. The foyer was dark with warm lighting that somehow made the room feel more cozier than Husher would have expected. The front desk fit the vibe of the rest of the place, dark wood on top, shiny and clean, and wrapped around the rest of it was galvanized steel that worked well with the dark colors of the entrance/front desk area.

"Good morning, Miss White," a woman in her mid-thirties greeted from behind the counter. Compared to the rest of the almost gothic decor and colors of the room her makeup was bright and vibrant, matching her purple hijab.

Husher looked around for a moment before turning back to the task at hand, forgetting why he was there for a second. He walked over to the counter but left Mason to do most of the talking since she had found the apartment and Husher knew next to nothing about what they would be needing or even what they would need to do before moving in. Jared was listening, so he could just ask him later if there was anything he needed to remember. It seemed like a foolproof plan to him.

"Morning, Lilya, we're here to pick up the keys," Mason said and put her arms on the counter, as if she was truly always comfortable in any element she was set in.

"Okay." The woman typed something into the computer before continuing, "Looks like you already sent over all the paperwork, I just need you all to sign one more thing and then I'll get the keys for you."

Husher zoned out for a moment waiting for her to get the paperwork, but Jared was nudging his arm to get his attention when it was his turn to sign. Husher signed what he needed to, and before he knew it they were walking up to their apartment. The hallway looked like it had been remodeled recently and their door was painted a shade of black.

Inside the apartment it was bright and like much more space than Husher had originally thought it would be like since Mason had refused to show them the pictures of the apartment beforehand. The apartment opened into the kitchen that doubled as the dining area, a good enough space for the three of them. The living room was right off from the kitchen, leaving a mostly open floor plan kind of feel to it. From the kitchen there were two hallways, a shorter one to the left that led to a half-bath and down farther to the largest of the bedrooms. The master bedroom had a full bath of its own along with a walk-in closet. It all seemed much nicer than Husher had been expecting. To the right of the kitchen and down the longer hallway were the other two bedrooms, both about the same size. The one to the left had the bigger closet of the two and the one on the right had better lighting. Both rooms led into the jack-and-jill bathroom between them.

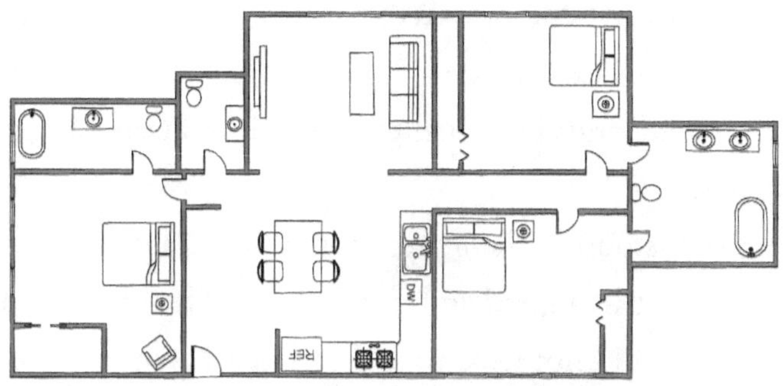

"I think it's safe to say who is getting which room," Mason stated.

"Dibs on the best windows," Jared raised his hand.

"Wow." Mason shook her head sarcastically. "I was going to pick that one."

Husher knew that was completely sarcastic since Mason normally had the blinds in her room closed all day. The only time she opened them was in the months of spring when she opened the windows.

In the end, they all agreed on which rooms they wanted. Mason took the biggest room, Jared took the room with the best lighting for his plants, and Husher got the one with the bigger closet, even though he knew Jared would most likely end up using half since the man had more clothes than Husher ever would.

"You love it?" Mason asked.

"Yes!" Jared exclaimed.

"It would kinda be difficult to not at least like it," Husher stated.

Husher stood in the living room looking out the window that let in a good amount of light. Then he caught himself; he did not need to add to Jared's plant addition by informing him they could get a narrow table and put a bunch of plants in front of the window. But the thought was still there that the window did in fact bring in enough light for his boyfriend's plant children.

"Good, because we have a two-year lease," Mason cheered. "Now we just, you know, have to unpack everything."

They spent the rest of the day moving into their apartment.

Most of what they had was brought from their old bedrooms and what Mason had gotten from the storage unit. Thankfully, Husher had cleaned the apartment a week ago with his mom, not knowing it would be the one that he would be moving into, so they at least didn't have to worry about it being gross from the last renters.

While Miss Moon was still at the diner for the day Husher's and Mason's parents helped them move in, and with Jason's truck getting the furniture was a lot quicker.

Husher was pretty sure his legs were going to fall off if he had to bring anything else up to the apartment. He and Mason had brought up all the boxes while their parents brought up the furniture, having to pivot the couch to even get it up the stairs.

"Wanna start with the kitchen to make everything livable?" Jared asked.

The apartment looked a bit overwhelming once they brought everything in, and while things were placed in the rooms they needed to be in to make it all less confusing and easier to deal with, it was all still a lot more than Husher would have thought.

"I can help you there," Husher's mom offered.

Jared nodded happily to not have to worry about someone—Husher—putting the supplies somewhere stupid like having the cups near the dishwasher and not near the fridge. Husher just moved out of their way after that. He helped Mason's dad put together the bed frames and the two nightstands he seriously thought would have taken less time for Jason to make on his own.

"I am fluent in two languages, and neither one is making these easier to read," Husher deadpanned.

"I started with the Spanish page but ended up switching to the English one, which was just as helpful," Jason exclaimed. "Pendejos don't even have good pictures."

"I have ten extra screws and I am pretty sure the back is on the wrong way," Husher said.

He looked over to the one Mason's dad built and it looked more like a nightstand with the normal extra amount of screws left off just in case.

"I don't think the drawer opens like that," Jason commented.

"There's a drawer?!" Husher looked back to the nightstand. "That would make a lot more sense."

By the time Husher and Jason got the nightstand taken apart and put back together the right way—or at least the less fucked up way Husher had it—the sun was setting and Husher was ready for bed.

Out in the rest of the apartment Jared and Husher's parents got most of the living room and kitchen put together nicely. A few things needed to be put up on the walls, but the kitchen was done at least. Husher and Jared ended up getting most of the kitchen supplies—except for the frog-themed blender—and they all agreed to split the cost of groceries until they came up with a system that would work for all of them.

It would be a great place for them to start college in a few days, and after the last few months, they all decided to take it slow for the first semester. Husher did not want to be more stressed out than the normal amount he usually was.

A knock on the door caught Husher off guard since most of the people he knew were already there.

"Someone get the door, I am hanging worms on my ceiling!" Mason shouted.

Husher seriously hoped she meant the worms on a string like the red one he wore as a neckless most of the time and not actual worms—the fact he had to question it was concerning on its own. She wouldn't hang live worms in her room... probably.

"I got it!" Husher shouted and made a mental note to make sure later.

Husher opened the door without looking to see who it was and his mom flicked him on the back of the head.

"I know you didn't just open the door without look-ing—also, hello Sally and Lee," Nicole said, moving out of the way.

Lee pushed their way in with a large bag behind them and a large iced orange juice in hand while Miss Moon brought several to-go bags with her. Husher could have hugged her then and there, but instead, he shut the door behind them and followed them to the kitchen.

"Hi?" Husher said, but it came out more like a question than anything else.

"Hey, dude." Lee put their stuff down on the edge of the couch and set their drink on the kitchen table. "I brought some housewarming things, and also I am inviting myself over for a much-needed sleepover. I am *not* asking."

Jared laughed. "You don't have to."

"True, and this gets me out of helping with dinner," Husher grinned.

Jared looked up, knife in hand. "Who said you get out of helping with dinner?"

"Come on, you know I'll do all the cleaning up to make it an even trade, and plus Miss Moon brought stuff." Husher pointed to the bags of food.

Lee pushed Husher out of the kitchen. "You know you're dating a fire hazard in the kitchen, or did you forget how he managed to cook the water out of a simple syrup?"

Jared cringed, clearly remembering leaving Husher alone for a few minutes to watch the sugar water mixture only to come back to the water boiling out of the sugar entirely and burning in the pot.

"You're right," Jared sighed. "I still don't understand how that happened though."

"None of us do," Ava pointed out.

"When did you get here?!" Husher whorled around to see his sister.

She rolled her eyes. "An hour ago with the extra bedding Mama asked me to bring, duh."

He just nodded in response before getting back to work, he wanted to get as much as he could done before the end of the night.

He had no problem getting lost in the tasks at hand.

By the time dinner was done, Husher had finished putting up the artwork in his room along with down the hallway that Jared and him both agreed on.

He hugged his parents, forcing himself not to cling to them to stay just a little longer. He even considered asking Ava to stay the night when he was hugging her goodbye but refrained and was glad whenever he later realized she put a: *'kick him, he's stupid'* note on his back that he only caught when Miss Moon had pointed it out. It did explain why Mason and Jared had kicked him earlier though.

Lee helped with adding the lights around the apartment which helped make it much cozier than it was before, Husher was delighted that Lee was staying over. Sleepovers were one of his favorite things, and he hoped to never grow out of it.

"So I heard something about housewarming gifts?" Mason asked.

Lee rolled their eyes and walked over to their bag. Husher had been too caught up with the food Miss Moon brought to remember Lee bringing gifts. They each were handed a small box and Lee chewed nervously at the side of their mouth. While gift-giving was their love language, they always thought that somehow whoever they were gifting was going to hate it. Husher knew he was a terrible gift giver—no matter how much thought, effort, planning, or love went into it he failed more times than he succeeded. Lee, however, was the opposite. They always had the perfect gift in mind for whoever it was and whatever the occasion was. They nailed it every time.

"It's just something small," Lee informed them, "but you can open them."

When Husher opened his there was a mix of his favorite things. His favorite strawberry-flavored candy, a red fuzzy blanket, and a manga he had been saying he wanted to read. He grinned at each item knowing he absolutely loved them all and how thoughtful Lee was for remembering the little things Husher rambled about. Like how he mentioned how he wished he just had a soft blanket that wasn't a boring color, but he could never find a red blanket that was soft enough.

"Thank you," Husher said sincerely.

Mason opened hers next. Which consisted of a green mushroom decoration, hot chocolate mix, and a custom green chain for her motorcycle.

"Wait, how?!" Mason screamed, looking down at the chain in disbelief.

"An elf has their ways," Lee answered. "I also had no idea what it was, so I asked Philip to order it in."

"So that was why he kept getting the packages at the shop." Mason nodded. "Thanks, bestie."

Husher looked over to see what his boyfriend got, and much like Mason and him, it was customized to his interests. Jared got a few seed packets for the herb garden he would put in near the window, two books that recently came out that he wanted, and of course a bat-themed mug.

"Thank you, Lee!" Jared smiled.

"Yeah, yeah, now I heard something about a sleepover," Lee smiled back.

Mason grinned. "I'll get the movies!"

When they all settled in the living room, Husher sat on the couch waiting as his friends all got more comfortable. Mason pressed play as the movie began, Lee set the bowls of popcorn on the table and Jared shoved Husher over making room for himself on the couch.

"Pink hearts or zombie boogers?" Jared asked, holding up two containers.

"Ooh give him the zombie one, it would be great for his pores," Mason muttered, mouth full of popcorn.

Husher scrunched up his face in confusion.

"Face masks," Jared muttered. Not waiting for an answer as he handed the pink container over to Mason and Jared opened the green one.

"You are not putting that on me."

Jared ignored him. "Close your eyes, bitch."

Husher looked to his boyfriend then back to the green goop he was trying to put onto his face. He weighed his options and closed his eyes.

"Good boy," Jared muttered, shoving a piece of popcorn in his mouth as a treat.

"You're an asshole!"

Jared hummed in agreement before he started applying the cold spa mask. Husher didn't hate it as much as he thought, nearly falling asleep by the time his boyfriend was done.

"So pretty," Mason muttered with a chuckle, "You look like something a kid picks out of their nose."

Husher opened his eyes sleepily.

Mason and Lee had the other mask on, looking just as odd as Husher assumed he did with the skincare stuff on.

"You want me to do yours?" Husher asked Jared.

"Shhh!" Mason shushed him.

Husher looked over to her. "You were just talking!"

She waved him off and Jared handed over the container and the small spoon he used to apply it. Jared put on the bat themed headband on, pulling his brown hair back. Husher was happy to see the freshly dyed parts of his hair. The sides shaved and dyed red once more. Jared sat a bit closer as he faced the blond to make it easier for him to see what he was doing.

Husher didn't pay attention to most of the movie as he slowly put the same mask onto his boyfriend. Sticking his tongue out slightly as he concentrated on not getting the spa mask in Jared's eyes or hair.

"You are not painting a picture dude," Jared chuckled.

Husher clutched his non-existent pearls for the millionth time. "Don't *dude* me."

Jared smirked, his eyes closed while Husher had been putting the mask on him. "Okay, *bestie*."

"You're a dick," Husher said jokingly.

"You both are," Mason muttered. "Shut up."

Husher rolled his eyes and finished up with the mask before setting it on the table. Jared handed him one of the bowls of popcorn.

"Thanks," Husher said, popping a piece into his mouth.

Jared nodded in acknowledgement.

It had taken all day, but Husher thought they did good with making the place their own. He was happy to be there with his friends.

Husher turned to see Jared looking at him and smirked. It was funny to think he never noticed that he liked him all those years and how now it felt no different than it had when they were just friends. Only now, they kissed and Husher was very much not complaining.

Jared turned away but Husher pulled him back and kissed him, no doubt messing up their spa masks he put on them. Husher didn't really mind when the familiar taste of marshmallow invaded his mouth, realizing that maybe home wasn't a place but rather a person.

"Gay!" Mason yelled.

Popcorn flew at them and they were forced to sit on opposite ends of the couch.

Jared laughed the whole time as Lee commented, "This is not the place to be whores. No shaming, I'm just saying."

Husher winked at his boyfriend and laughed at how quickly Jared blushed and had to turn back to the movie.

The screams filling the living room from the TV should not have felt as comforting as it did, but Husher wouldn't trade it for anything. He was right where he belonged: with his friends.

THE END

Raspberry "Cinnamon" Roll Recipe

Ingredients:

All-Purpose Flour (or Bread Flour)

Sugar

Butter

Egg

Yeast

Water

Milk

Salt

Frozen Raspberries

Brown Sugar

Ground Cinnamon

Vanilla Extract

Powdered/Confectioners Sugar

Dough:

2 ¾ cups all-purpose flour or bread flour (340 to 350g)

¼ cup of sugar (56g)

2 tablespoons of butter (30g)

1 egg

2 ¼ tsp yeast (1 packet, 7g)

½ cup <u>warm</u> water (118ml)

¼ <u>warm</u> milk cup (59ml)

1 tsp salt

Filling:

1 cup raspberries (125g)

⅔ cup brown sugar (149g)

½ <u>softened</u> stick butter (56g)

1 tbsp ground cinnamon (15g)

1 tsp vanilla extract (5ml)

Glaze:

1 ½ cups of powdered/confectioners sugar (190g)

½ stick butter <u>melted</u> (56g)

1 tsp vanilla extract (5ml)

2 tbsp milk (30ml)

Steps:

Take ½ cup of water and ¼ of milk and put in the microwave for 30 seconds or until the mixture is warm—NOT HOT.

In a large/medium bowl add the water and milk mixture. 1 teaspoon of sugar, and 2 ¼ teaspoons of yeast (or 1 packet). Whisk together then let it sit for 5-10 minutes, until it doubles in size.

In a different bowl add 2 ¾ cups of all-purpose (or bread) flour and 1 teaspoon of salt. Mix together with a whisk.

Microwave 2 tablespoons of butter.

Once the yeast has proofed add in the melted butter and the rest of the sugar and then whisk again.

Add in 1 large egg and whisk it all together. Put in the mixer (or mix by hand) and add in the flour (slowly) and save ⅓ cup flour for later. Knead the dough for 8 minutes, using the rest of the flour.

Oil (or spray) a big bowl and transfer the dough there with plastic wrap and a clean dish towel covering the top. Leave to sit for 1 hour to rest.

Drain 1 cup of frozen raspberries (or if using fresh, wash them thoroughly) before adding in ½ cup of sugar and 1 teaspoon of vanilla extract. Mix them in a medium bowl.

After the dough has rested, roll it out and over it in softened butter. Add raspberry mix. Roll up the dough into a log, then cut with a knife or with dental floss.

Spray (or butter) a pan and add the rolls. Cover the rolls again with plastic wrap and a clean dish towel and let them rest for another 1 hour.

Brush the rolls with melted butter before putting them in the oven at 375°F (or 190°C) for 15-20 minutes.

Let the rolls cool down for about 10 minutes. Make simple icing on top (or leave it as is).

Mix 1 ½ cups of powdered/confectioner's sugar (190g), ½ stick butter <u>melted</u> (56g), 1 tsp vanilla extract (5ml), and 2 tbsp milk (30ml) in a bowl until all combined.

Pour glaze over the raspberry cinnamon rolls.

Lastly, enjoy!

Author's Note

Thank you for taking the time to read this book!! I hope it was at the very least entertaining and if not, well, there isn't really anything I can do about it now that you've already read it so this is a bit awkward *(for you)*.

Consider leaving a review, on Amazon, Goodreads, StoryGraph and/or wherever else you post book reviews, it would be greatly appreciated; they are extremely important in general but especially helpful for self-published books. Even if you hated it and want to curse about it in the wind, I'd love to see the support bestie.

-Dustin Mars

About the Author

Dustin Mars, friend to some, enemy to most, is from somewhere in the mountains of Pennsylvania where cicadas sing and cryptids lurk. When he's not writing he can be found wandering into the void of nothing, listening to the same song on repeat until it's hated, or staying up into the morning hours reading on Ao3. Dustin enjoys spending time away from as many people as possible and he dies inside every time small talk is involved.

9 798991 844345